THE OTHER SIDE OF

CARAF Books
Caribbean and African Literature Translated from French
Renée Larrier and Mildred Mortimer, Editors

THE OTHER SIDE OF THE SEA

LOUIS-PHILIPPE DALEMBERT

Translated by Robert H. McCormick Jr.

Foreword by Edwidge Danticat

University of Virginia Press
Charlottesville and London

Originally published in French as *L'Autre Face de la mer*
(Éditions Stock, 1998)
© 1998 by Louis-Philippe Dalembert

University of Virginia Press
Translation and foreword © 2014 by the Rector and Visitors
of the University of Virginia
All rights reserved
Printed in the United States of America on acid-free paper

First published 2014

9 8 7 6 5 4 3 2 1

LIBRARY OF CONGRESS CATALOGING-IN-PUBLICATION DATA
Dalembert, Louis-Philippe.
  [Autre Face de la mer. English]
  The other side of the sea / Louis-Philippe Dalembert ; translated by
Robert H. McCormick Jr. ; foreword by Edwidge Danticat.
      pages   cm.—(Caribbean and African literature translated from
French)
  ISBN 978-0-8139-3646-8 (cloth : alk. paper)—ISBN 978-0-8139-3647-5
(pbk. : alk. paper)—ISBN 978-0-8139-3648-2 (e-book)
  1. Haiti—Fiction. I. McCormick, Robert H., 1944– translator. II. Title.
  PQ3949.2.D25A9413 2014
  843'.914—dc23

                                                    2014024530

Cover art: Maria Meester/Shutterstock

CONTENTS

FOREWORD

Louis-Philippe Dalembert is one of the most imaginative and prolific writers of his generation. Born in Port-au-Prince, Haiti, in 1962, he calls himself a "vagabond," or nomad, in honor of all the places he has lived and worked. There is of course Haiti, where he spent his childhood and early adulthood, and there is Paris, where he studied journalism and where he still resides part of the year. He has had stays at the prestigious Villa Medici in Rome, as well as at artists' colonies in Berlin, and much shorter stays in Jerusalem, Egypt, Jordan, and elsewhere.

Dalembert writes in many genres. He is a poet, short story writer, and playwright, as well as a novelist. He can express himself in seven languages. He writes in both French and Haitian Creole. Just as he has a wanderer's curiosity about the world, he is equally curious about various forms and structures and ways of telling a story. His work is hard to pin down because he himself is hard to pin down. He displays just as much confidence mimicking the village griot as he does the ivory tower philosopher. To use a Haitian expression for restless travelers, his feet are *poudre,* or "powdered," as much with village dust as with pixie dust. And this is why he is the perfect novelist to take on this physical and psychological journey *lòt bò dlo,* or to the other side of the sea.

The author of eight novels, three collections of short stories, four volumes of poetry, and one book of reportage, Dalembert has been widely profiled or had his work reviewed in publications ranging from *Le Monde Diplomatique* to *World Literature Today.* He has won a slew of prizes, including the 2008 Casa de las Américas Prize. It is surprising that his work has not been translated into English until now. But here he is, at last, thanks to this translation by Robert McCormick, and for that, I am very grateful.

I came across Dalembert's work through his first novel, pub-

FOREWORD

lished in 1996, *Le crayon du Bon Dieu n'a pas de gomme,* or *God's pencil has no eraser.* By then he had already published a collection of stories called *Le songe d'une photo d'enfance,* or *Dream of a childhood photo.* I remember losing myself in the stunning and poetic language of *Le crayon du Bon Dieu,* a story set in a fictional version of Haiti, with its imaginary capital Port-aux-Grimes. The characters in that book were wild, innocent, colorful, but always real, even as they floated, wandered, or got lost in their own enchanted worlds.

How do we call a place home when there are nothing but dreams and fragments of memory tying us to that place? Dalembert seems to be posing that question over and over again. His characters are constantly moving, traveling from one location to the next, be it from the provinces to the capital, between cities, or from one country to another. Even when they are not traveling, they are dreaming about it, all the while looking closely at portals to other places: camions, airplanes, the sea. Child narrators are often difficult to write well, but Dalembert seems to take pleasure in them, which made that book exquisitely captivating and immediately turned me into a huge fan of his work.

Reading that first novel also reminded me of the connections between Dalembert and a writer on whose work he wrote his doctoral dissertation, the Cuban Alejo Carpentier. Both Carpentier and Dalembert are lyrical and efficient writers who pack a lot of story into a small space. Carpentier too was a *pye poudre,* a restless wanderer, who worked in many literary genres and had a penchant for musicality in his language. And one can sometimes sense elements of Carpentier's *real maravilloso,* or real marvelous—his precursor to magical realism—in Dalembert's work. Not necessarily in tropical hat tricks, but in the ways that the color of the sea abruptly changes, or a character's dreams come to life, or that a character suddenly reveals himself to be something other than what we thought him or her to be.

The past, too, is never too far away, both the distant past of the native Tainos and their encounter with Columbus and one of a more recent dictatorial dynasty. Whether narrated by a great-uncle, or a child, or a novelist trying to write the story we're reading, history is always present. Human beings are either trapped by history or are trying to escape it, but they can never ignore it, even when they might want to. And Dalembert does not want to. In both developing an ingenious plot and showing the way events took place, he lays everything bare, pulling back the veil in a way that, surprisingly, intensifies our suspension of disbelief. Here Dalembert the journalist surfaces. He is our ally, our eyes, and we believe and trust him. With a writer like Dalembert, we always know we are in capable narrative hands.

The Other Side of the Sea is Dalembert's second novel. Published in 1998, it seems to have had its genesis in the title story of his first story collection, *Le songe d'une photo d'enfance*. In the novel, as well as in the short story collection, many are fleeing, leaving the world they know behind. In Haitian parlance, when a person is said to have gone *lòt bò dlo*, or to have gone to the other side of the water, that person has either migrated or died. This book takes into account all those deaths—the physical ones on land and at sea as well as the psychological deaths, the ones that precede and follow departures, the endless humiliations at the consulates, the selling or bartering of every material good, even if it means never looking back, "for fear of being turned into statues of salt."

The Other Side of Sea is a novel told in several voices. We have the grandmother, the memory keeper, the community elder, the *poto mitan*, the one who will not leave. We also have her grandson Jonas, who represents the new generation, the one whose lack of opportunities and sense of adventure make him think of nothing but leaving. Set between these voices is that of a third-person narrator who provides a broader view, who summarizes for us the history of these characters' place and time. In the midst of all this are woven in stream-of-consciousness fragments, an effect that mirrors the way the characters are actually thinking. Through these various accounts, we learn about four generations of one family. Their migrations also echo general Haitian migration patterns. Grannie, we learn, has survived the 1937 massacre of Haitians in the neighboring Dominican Republic. Her recollections of her harrowing escape add an element of adventure to the novel. However, this is not the type of adventure that young men (or women) generally seek, and it is not the type of adventure that she would wish on her grandson or anyone else.

Jonas, though, is less tempted by working in the sugarcane fields and more by the lights of big cities farther away. He is also torn about the realities of the city in which he lives and the daily hardships it imposes on its citizens. Would it make a difference if he stayed? Or is he just one pebble in sinking sand, someone who can be lynched at the drop of a hat and have his charred remains turned over to hungry pigs? The only person to whom his life seems to truly matter is his grandmother, who has nothing to offer him but her story and her prayers.

The sea, Grannie's constant focal point, looms large in the novel. The Haitian expression "Naje pou soti" literally means "swim your way out." Though its meaning is closer to "sink or swim," the more literal version rings a lot more true on an island where thousands have taken to the seas to escape both extreme poverty and political repression. Or, in Jonas's words, "Entire families had constructed lightweight boats that could barely manage to stay above water. . . . Quite often, the fragile skiffs capsized a few miles farther out, overturned by the first groundswell or the first reef encountered. The sea would open, swallow the passengers, then close up over them before regaining its indolence. No survivors."

The sea's indolence and its timelessness are endlessly fascinating to Grannie. The sea is perhaps one of the few things that has always been there for her and will always be. And because she has stopped seeing it as a means of physical escape, she is able to revel in it as a place of imagination and memory, even a sacred space. Besides, if everyone takes to the seas and swims to the Promised Land, who will be left behind to remember? Who will be left to tell the stories?

This novel, like Dalembert's other work, is full of biblical references. In addition to the above reference to Lot's wife and the pillar of salt, the name Jonas itself alludes to the book of Jonah, in which Jonah takes to the seas and is swallowed by a great whale. Our Jonas's Nineveh, his great and glorious city, is the "Promised-Land-in-Spite-of-Itself." Will he suffer the same

FOREWORD

fate as the biblical Jonah, but minus the miraculous ending? That seems to be his grandmother's greatest fear.

Grannie's ultimate journey, however, like all of ours, is beyond her control. And to some extent so is Jonas's. His search to overcome that powerlessness is what drives him. And unlike his grandmother, he potentially has more living ahead of him than behind him. "Life and death are two sides of the same coin," he eventually realizes. "In the course of one and the same life, we don't stop dying: we're always afraid, always suffering. Unless we prefer a sojourn without surprises and refuse all invitations from the world beyond. . . . On the other side of the ocean."

Dalembert echoed that same sentiment in a poem published in January 2013. In "Port-au-Prince on an IV Drip," he writes, "everyman's life slips away / if we knew how to count / we'd already be far." Jonas's and Grannie's journeys show that the way we count—and recount—is just as essential as the sum of our lives. A valuable lesson that we, readers of this marvelous book, are also left to cling to.

THE OTHER SIDE OF THE SEA

In memory of Kiki
For Caétan and Pia

So they became fugitives and wanderers; it was said among the nations, "They shall stay here no longer."

—Lamentations 4:15

Then there were all those departures and all those renounce-ments: those who left and those who stayed. Those who left not having been able to stay, those who stayed not having been able to leave, those who left for not having dared to stay, for fear of dying or coming up with their daily bread; and those who left like that, to leave, to not be there any longer . . .

—*Et le soleil se souvient*

GRANNIE'S STORY

For a long time, I've dreamt of crossing the ocean, like you would step over a puddle of water, to see the point where the earth and sky meet, the very roots of the horizon. An old dream of youth, now beyond my reach . . . Jonas better not hear me; otherwise, I'd be entitled to a good scolding. "Stop talking nonsense, Grannie." Anyone but him would have already faced the facts. The wheel has turned. The other side of life is waiting for me, and I am approaching the shore without regrets . . .

As children, we lived in a neighborhood on the top of a hill, a sort of roof of the city, and of the world, from which I could follow the slightest undulation of the ocean before the cities of cardboard, of rusty sheet metal, and of mud came and obstructed the view. Having ignored my parents' ban, rushing down to the docks and dodging in and out between the carriages and the first automobiles was child's play that only became perilous at the thought, too often realized, of getting a beating upon my return. Still out of breath from the climb, no sooner had I planted my feet on the veranda than a hand would grab me and make me pay, in cash, the expenses of my escapade. But while Madame Lorvanna was beating me, more by habit than by the conviction of succeeding one day in eradicating my vice, and my body was deceptively twisting so that she would stop taking me for a drum, my mind was flying a thousand miles away, transported by a nursery rhyme that my classmates and I had invented on the playground to defy the rules of the adults. It was enough to hum it to yourself mentally, sometimes even audibly, as a provocation, to become insensitive to the punishment inflicted and ready to renew your crime.

> Kale m, kale m, kale m!
> Kò m se zèb, la pouse.

So, I often found myself on the docks witnessing the departure and the arrival of the cargo ships. I was indifferent to the comings and goings of the dockworkers sweating and laboring under the sacks of sugar, coffee, and cocoa. My attention was scarcely diverted by the crowd of well-dressed people gathered on the platform: some waiting for a relative, for a friend returning from overseas, some, between two sobs or with an impassive countenance suppressing their pain, having come to wish a safe journey to someone close to them. With increasing excitement, I scrutinized the appearance of the first arrivals, although, truth be told, those leaving attracted me just as much. I would have liked to have gone up to them and asked them what they had brought back from over there. From the other side of the horizon. Not those external signs of the grand crossing, that more than one but-have-you-seen flaunted to elicit their neighbors' jealousy. Such trinkets have never interested me. I would have liked for them to recount their experiences, to tell me about the differences encountered, the sweet incomprehension of new languages, the flowers, the trees, the snow . . . all that rendered over there so beautiful.

Those semi-clandestine visits to the docks were like a piggy bank into which I deposited all the riches of my imagination. A treasure gleaned here and there with the excitement and the perseverance of a collector. No piece of information escaped my curiosity. Besides the old half-torn magazines that fell into my hands under circumstances I could no longer explain and that I devoured with the slow appetite of a man condemned to death, I didn't miss a single geography class. Thus, I became the teachers' pet, and they would often let me lead the recitation.

Today, it would be difficult for me to say what that other side of the world I dreamt about looked like. There were so many of them. So many and so many and so many. Each one always different from the others. It depended on my imagination. And on the weather that day (sometimes the boats resisted the most ferocious hurricanes; sometimes they slid along like swans on the calmest of seas). From conversations picked up from the people around me, a word seized in passing, and my imagination started running at full speed, populating those distant lands with all the whims of a dreamy little girl. What was the Amazon forest of my childhood composed of? What kinds of imaginary beings lived there? The shifting sand dunes of the Sahara, the Promised Land, the great Australia inhabited by myriads of kangaroos . . .

"Look, one day, when you aren't expecting it, you will disappear, you yourself, into your eyes-wide-open-dreams."

The phrase was Hermanos's (one of my four brothers, twin of Jacques-Antonio, younger brother of Diogène and Pétion), jealous of not being able to penetrate into my secret garden. It annoyed him to see me close the two panels of the door and leave, like that, without his knowing where my imagination had taken me. But I didn't pay any attention to it because I liked Hermanos, a lot even. And since he alone was denied entrance into my dreams, I continued to embark for even more distant shores that I was the first to marvel at.

It's funny, I feel the same strange sensation going back to all those recollections in the deepest recesses of my memory. A sensation that, who knows why, frightens and gives pleasure at the same time. Like when I heard the sound of the horn, coming from the boat indicating its departure, piercing the air, imposing silence on the population. Everything seemed paralyzed: the noise of the horseshoes on the cobblestones, the activity of the stevedores, the raucous flight of the seagulls, the indecisive arabesques of the clouds, the laughter and the tears . . . letting the deafening sound invade the whole world of things. Only the roaring that regulated the labor of the sugarcane workers, and seemed to come from the smoked-filled mouth of the factory's immense smokestack, had a power as paralyzing. And when the first moment of stupor had passed, while the white handkerchiefs were being waved at arms' end, the animation timidly resumed. Perched up on my clouds, I saw the ship pull away from the landing stage with deafening rumblings, distance itself from the pier, merge like a grain of sand into the horizon, and then disappear from my sight, leaving me as dismayed as if the love of my life had been taken away on board.

In the meantime, the onlookers and escorts had deserted the docks. Only a few dockworkers, who were finishing up their showers with the help of a rubber hose, remained. Having just arrived, the fried-fish vendors were unpacking their paraphernalia, setting up their stalls and starting, in turn, their workday. Soon thereafter the few streetlights, which the city had recently provided to replace the oil lamps, went on, delivering the streets

10

THE OTHER SIDE OF THE SEA

to a mob of people whose habits were unknown to me at my
young age. Executed with habit's detachment, those maneuvers
brought me abruptly back down to earth: it was time to take to
my heels and make my way back home. Returning, I brought,
with my facial expression, all the elsewhere suggested by the
ship's departure. Then Hermanos shot me an angry glance.

"You'll see, you'll end up disappearing into your dreams,
you little idiot, and no one will be able to bring you back."

Only Diogène had the gift of driving me up the wall when he
felt like it. All he had to do was to say to me, "A new boat has
arrived at the port, one you have never seen." And without worrying about the presence or the absence of Mama Lorvanna, I
would fly off like an arrow, beating even the speed of the wind.
Generally, once on the spot, I would realize that it was an old
cargo ship that a simple glance from the top of the hill would
have enabled me to identify. And while I was returning on the
sly, completely out of breath because of my arrow-like round
trip, he would call out to me while bursting out laughing, "Did
you see the *new boat*?" Even though I'd sworn to myself that
he would never catch me again, my curiosity and his deceit won
out over my resolution every time. The one time I succeeded
in not giving in—it was raining cats and dogs that day, so I
had a good pretext for not rushing outside, needlessly, before
returning as drenched as a duck—I lost the chance to admire
an exact replica of the *Titanic* that was anchored in the bay. It
was the property of a German multimillionaire who was doing
a port-to-port around-the-world tour. Since then, scarcely had
Diogène uttered his *"new boat"* than I would fly off the handle.
That's how I inherited the nickname that people here would
transform into Noubòt. In time, my grandson, Jonas, has taken
over from my two brothers, pulling me out of my daydreaming
with a "What are you dreaming about again, dear Grannie?"
Luckily, God gave him to me, that one.

||||||||||||||||||||||||||||||||||||||||||||||||||||||||||||||||||||||||||||||||||||||||||||||||||||||||||||||

the big boat is there waiting for them the livestock are advancing toward it hundreds of animals cross one after the other the
narrow corridor that leads to it the eyes empty of all expression

without understanding what is happening to them the passage
narrows at the level of the junction between the bulkhead and
hull not larger than the shoulders of the smallest among them
the most robust must proceed at an angle a kick or a rifle butt to
the scapula facilitate the progress of those who rear up afraid

in the flank of the big boat a gate opens that leads directly
to the hold there the livestock are separated into two or three
levels sardined sausaged not a moan escapes from their mouths
the gate closes infernal noise the obscurity has swallowed them

the big boat casts off they are there pallid the moorings cast
off the sails hoisted toward the unknown for which they embark millions of others before them have made the same trip
without end today it's their turn in the night the bodies in the
hold are touching each other to the point where it hurts do the
animals know how to cry the big boat casts off toward nonexistent elsewhere after them there will be others millions of others

|||||||||||||||||||||||||||||||||||||||||||||||||||||||||||||||||||||||||||||||||||||||||||||||||||||||||||||||||||||||||||||

Why, one might say, that virtually obsessive desire to cross the
ocean? It's difficult to explain all that to someone. All my life,
the ocean's never stopped taunting me, approaching the horizon, then moving away the moment I finally thought I could
touch it. Even today, it makes my blood boil, although the doctor, because of my heart, recommended that I avoid all forms
of irritation. And my little Jonas who comes up to me: "Stop
worrying, Grannie." But how can you not be irritated at seeing
it immured in its arrogance? Sometimes calm and silver, brown-
ing its stomach like a lizard in the sun. Not even condescending
to look at you. Sometimes gray and rough, controlling neither
its excesses nor its howling. Sticking its tongue out as if to say:
"No one will tame me." Inaccessible. And suddenly, its desire to
take you, to slip into the most intimate part of your suffering.
How many times has it battered this city, after having leapt over
the railing, invaded the streets, penetrated the houses without
respect for anyone! Then, it pulls back with the same noncha-
lance. You might think that it was insuperable and couldn't be
straddled like an ordinary ditch.

I wasn't unaware that it was possible. Christopher Columbus had successfully arrived here by sea, I repeated to persuade myself. The whites, too, whose accomplice he was, casting them onto our shores one afternoon when the whole town was taking its siesta. I was sitting outside, not letting it out of my sight, when I noticed an unusual activity at the port. I leapt quickly over the balustrade, rushed down the hill, and ended up not far from the docks when I saw them taking possession of the area cobblestone by cobblestone. They had arrived with big olive-green cars made of steel, mounted on a thousand legs like caterpillars, that I had never seen before. They were turning their heads in all directions, pointing at the houses their long, terrifying muzzles that spat death over a distance of several kilometers.

I was so terrified by the harshness of their stares that I took the same path back, without the usual stop half-way up the middle of the hill, and arrived back home with my tongue hanging out. I woke Papa and everyone in the house with him: "Papa, there are white policemen at the port. White policemen are at the port. Policemen . . ." Without even asking me where I had gotten such information, he took on an aggressive demeanor, set off like a shot for the veranda, and understood immediately what was going on. He promptly reentered the living room, took an old machete down from the wall that no one could attest to having seen him use, and would have left to confront the foreign policemen if Mama hadn't held him back, using the dual persuasiveness of her hands and her tears. But he was furious: "The whites are in the city. I can't stay here and not do anything." If he finally ended up listening to reason, it's because he changed temperament from one day to the next, withering like a thirsty bush over the course of weeks.

As for the whites, they would stay in the city for a whole generation. They had serious expressions on their faces. They were arrogant, disrupting our customs without excusing themselves, putting everyone on the military rhythm of their language (the *"new boat"* of Diogène hadn't unfortunately made me used to those guttural sounds that were jostled together without any charm when they spoke). They had imposed their language on us from the first years of primary school; whereas, before they

disembarked, it was studied at the secondary level. I suspected
them of wanting to substitute it for French, for the beautiful
fables of La Fontaine and others like "Rodrique, do you have
the courage?" that we took such pleasure in reciting under the
attentive eye, and ear, of the teacher. The first lesson had started
with our learning the words of their national anthem, a fact
that set me against them even more. I refused to learn it, preferring the spankings of the teacher (I didn't have much choice).
Sometimes, to allay suspicion, I pretended to follow attentively,
when in fact, I would drift far away from the class and its stupid
droning. How could you appreciate the language of someone
who was conducting himself as supreme commander in someone else's house?

I quickly found an ally in the person of Papa, who was becoming more and more surly. All he had to do was run into one
of the foreign policemen on his route for him to be choked with
anger, even after having changed sidewalks. He would then return to the house and declare, point-blank, to Mama: "I'm leaving. Since those guys with the tomato faces set foot in this city,
it feels like a prison." We other kids, we would laugh because
he wouldn't stop repeating that refrain without, for an instant,
letting us imagine that he would act on his threat.

Truth be told, this city has always seemed like a prison to me.
Who wouldn't feel like a prisoner seeing the ocean nibble away
all day long at the space Christians need so as not to live one
on top of the other like young goats. Now that I have turned
my back on convention and have gotten closer to the essence
of things, my legs wouldn't even permit me to escape to the top
of the surrounding hills, scaling them like a buck rabbit. And
then, once up there, what else would I see but water as far as
the eye could see? Water diminishing my land and increasing
the distance that separates it from the world. I'm telling you, the
ocean, it's like bars that let you catch a glimpse of the wings
of liberty without being able to embrace the horizon for an instant. Even if you cling to them, try to demolish them, it's never
anything but useless sweat. The only thing you get is bloody
hands and broken fingers.

THE OTHER SIDE OF THE SEA

When I was a kid—even into my adolescence, by the way—I would often wake up with a start, wresting my mind out of an atrocious nightmare. A gigantic dam breaks, liberating hundreds of thousands of cubic meters of water into the city. It's run for your life. The liquid mass is advancing at the speed of lightning, pulverizing everything in its path. Since it's coming from the east, the whole city starts running toward the west, toward the ocean. I synchronize my steps with those of the crowd, but, after a certain time, I realize that I'm running alone. In spite of my panic, I continue running; it even stimulates me. I run, I run, I run. I'm several strides from the wharf when the ocean towers up in front of me. A wall more imposing than that of Jericho. Behind it, the squall is approaching with a staggering roar. I am going to be crushed, flattened like a cassava without any witnesses to bring the news of my death to my family. They would at least come to toss some flowers on the indifferent waves. And at the moment when the first waves are licking my feet, I wake up abruptly, summoned by a voice seeming to come from behind the wall . . . in fact, by my own cries. The next day, my older sister Luciana, who shared the room with me, took her revenge for losing a good third of a night's sleep by making me trot like a mule on the way to school.

The whites ended up finding a place for themselves on our landscape, with Papa's admonitions constituting the sound track. I didn't have the time, though, to put them on the same plane as the ocean; destiny had decided differently. A long time afterward, winding and unwinding the web of events that followed, I succeeded in elucidating certain signs that at the time were beyond my comprehension. Of course, the presence of the whites exasperated Papa so much so as to push him into action, but that was just the last straw. The idea—one had to face the facts—had been running through his head for quite a while already, well before their arrival. If not, why then would he spend hours on Sunday mornings fiddling with the radio until he came across those syrupy songs—years later I learned they were rancheras—he would listen to with the look of someone who had planted his feet in another world? A sort of first taste of paradise. Anyone who bothered him during those moments was in for it! Why were the twins called Hermanos and Antonio, my elder sister, Luciana? And many other indications of that nature that I learned to decipher with a detective's patience. For example, the disappearance of such and such a neighbor about whom a quick inquiry revealed that he had left *pa'lá,* meaning to the other side of the mountains.

For a long time, I wanted to cross out that chapter of our history, dig a big hole in my memory, throw it in there, then cover it back up with minor quotidian facts, with scraps of other stories, even the least interesting. What's the point in dwelling on bitterness? But bad seeds die hard. The more I repressed it, the more it would resurface, contaminating other stories I was telling, integrate itself into my words like a tapeworm into the intestines. What happened over there? I still can't talk about it in a coherent way. And besides, rehashing the thousand and one episodes of our odyssey, I would only be adding a personal note to a collective drama. Everything has been said, written, and sung about it: the cruelty of the soldiers over there, the cowardice of our politicians then, the 25,000 deniers of shame, our legitimate indignation . . . What one neglects to underscore sometimes is the noble solidarity of those men and women thanks to whom our lives were saved.

In short, it's old, all that. Dozens of hurricanes have passed over: Inès, Flora, Hazel, I am forgetting some and not the least of them. Even the three very recent ones, which are finally starting to bear the names of men: David, Hugo . . . It's the rightful evolution of things, isn't it? As if everything injurious in the world was caused only by women. If we are to believe those morons who baptize them, hurricanes are as whimsical and unpredictable as we are. The story of the apple already riles me. If I still tolerate it somewhat, that's because it comes from the Book of Books. And on top of that, they blame us for hurricanes!

By the way, you don't have to have exhausted your brain and your eyes in interminable study at elite universities to under-

stand that this region has a problem. One day, it's a storm that
ushers the ocean and squalls of rain into your home, without
asking your permission, uproots hundred-year-old mapou trees
that, until then, had known how to resist the destructive power
of men. Another day, a volcano spews its lava in your face.
Then an earthquake comes like a thief at night and surprises
you when you're sound asleep, shaking even a monumental
fortress like an ordinary coconut tree. Here, at least, we only
have to deal with hurricanes, a little jolt from time to time, and
hunger that advances with large strides and will end up eating
us all. Perhaps even before the ocean. In my family, you can
say Eben-Ezer! Up till now, Eternal God has helped us. Those
scourges aside, few natural calamities. There are no more trees?
Let's be honest. We didn't just get up one fine morning and find
the desert, brought by imaginary enemies, at our doorsteps . . .

How had I landed there? Once again, I let my mind wander.
At a certain age, you know, your head, it's like a boat whose
compass you've lost. But okay, I'm rambling too much. Quiet,
mouth! Let's go straight to the point, without those lovers'
tricks that get you from a distance to bring you in close, and
you find yourself in positions that you hadn't at all foreseen. At
least, not as fast as him.

What was Papa hoping to find on the other side of the moun-
tain chain? Certainly not El Dorado, for our situation here was
far better than the destiny that was waiting for us over there.
He and Mama were working, and we had never lacked anything. The house we were living in was modest, to be sure, but
it belonged to us. Why, once we were there, seeing the shack
where we were going to live—the matting full of bugs—hadn't
they turned around and gone back the way they came? And
why did Mama only tell us the night before that we were leaving the next day and wake us up before dawn to leave on the sly,
without me having been able to say good-bye to my friends? I
was still half asleep when I had to take on a bundle as heavy as
a sack of salt, taken over grudgingly by a grumpy Hermanos,
who didn't dare show his discomfort out loud for fear of getting
a slap, which would have succeeded in waking both of us up.

GRANNIE'S STORY

Two donkeys were waiting for us in the plain on the edge of town that we reached at the end of an hour or two of walking. An interminable time, in any case, because we had to advance at a tortoise's pace and be careful where we put our feet in the dark.

We quickly put our heaviest things in shoulder sacks. The sun was already rising when we set out again along paths I didn't even know existed. To say that the trip was exhausting would be a euphemism. Two days and two nights through woods, thickets, and mountains under a sun that literally peeled the skin off your head. And it never stopped. The hardest part was finding yourself on the crests of the hills with the sun beating down, beating down, beating down. How was it that none of us got sunstroke? Our bodies were dripping, the sweat blurred our vision, and our kneecaps were scraping the ground. That's where all my body fat melted and I took on the silhouette of smoked herring that I am known for.

||||||||||||||||||||||||||||||||||||||||||||||||||||||||||||||||||||||||||||||||||||||||||||||||||||||||||||||||||||||||||

the big boat left the coast one day ago and its night perhaps two perhaps three in steerage time confused mixing up the day and the night in the same mass of shadows the livestock head to tail intertwined contorted reduced to the most economical geometric figures just space enough for air to filter through shadowy steerage smells stuffy

above the noise of steps running in a thunderous coming and going of people who work at slower almost relaxed rhythms others who stroll stop no doubt leaning on the railing exchanging shouts now and then in unknown languages from the hold the livestock whose eyes learn to see in the permanent night and the waves bang against the hull of the big boat the whistling of the wind in the sails where is it going its destination no doubt escapes the livestock below how many days for the crossing time suspended except for the darkness

||||||||||||||||||||||||||||||||||||||||||||||||||||||||||||||||||||||||||||||||||||||||||||||||||||||||||||||||||||||||||

During that period, no one would have known how to remove from peoples' minds here the idea that one could easily make a fortune on the other side of the border. It was enough, they thought, to cross the Massacre River . . . Upon our arrival there, no one was waiting for us: neither an immense crowd gathered at the base of a footbridge nor a welcoming committee to ask us if we had had a good trip. That was for me the first disappointment. The situation was already tense: we were going to live there in a gigantic open-air concentration camp under the surveillance of armed men who didn't seem to have a sense of humor. All of that didn't become clear to me until later, for it would have taken much more than that to prevent us kids from basking in the carefree nature of our everyday life.

More resourceful than anyone else, Papa found a job on a plantation very quickly. There is no stupid job, he grumbled, as if to justify himself. From sunrise until nightfall cutting sugarcane, in the midst of big red ants that devoured your legs, of leaves whose edges were sharper than a razor blade and would lacerate your arms and face. The euphoria of the first days having faded, he would return worn out at night. His body was covered with pustules that he would spend the night scratching before a *viejo,* a former cane worker, advised him to rub aloe on it, the gluey sap of which reduced the itching. He scarcely spoke a word to us, let alone put me on his knees and bounce me up and down as I liked. He limited himself to swallowing, without a word, the rice and beans that Mama had prepared before lying down on our common mat. Sometimes he would remain with his eyes open in the dark, stretched out on his back thinking about God knows what remorse.

With the work, the plantation's administration had assigned a small, dilapidated shack to Papa that threatened to collapse at any minute, like that old tower, the image of which I saw once in a history book. We had to constantly prop it up for fear that it would fall in on top of us while we were sleeping. The boys succeeded quite well in doing that, I must admit. Ordinarily, we only found ourselves together in our one room to sleep, after having stayed up until the last flicker of the candle. Obliged to go to bed early because of the absence of electricity, we woke up when the sky, a witness of my horrible quarrels with Pétion, was growing pale. While sleeping, he thought he was a horse and let fly with solid kicks that, every time, reached the chest of his neighbor, in this case me and only me. That annoying habit had induced the family to relegate him to the extreme edge of the mat, where, besides the boards that he made screech all night long, I was the only one next to him. The hardest was when it rained, when the whole family had to squeeze into the shack for the entire day. That would end in horrible quarrels with Mama Lorvanna in the middle trying to calm the storm.

Mama had begun to gather together assorted objects to start a retail store. The former seamstress from the seaside didn't know how to remain inactive for long. In any case, my father's weekly salary wouldn't have provided for our needs. As for us, well, we spent our days provoking each other while waiting to be able to go to school. One of the commanders had promised it to my father after having decided that Pétion and Diogène were—a quick glance at their frames of twelve and thirteen years sufficed—capable of using a machete against the cane stalks. My father started to protest that his sons wouldn't take to that wretched profession. He wanted to make lawyers and doctors of them, at the very worst, teachers (which was what Antonio ended up becoming). The veins in his neck ready to explode, Papa was seething with anger when the commander, for whom there was no complaining, had already turned on his heels. But Papa didn't know how to say all that in their language. And besides, he had understood that his refusal would have brought about the immediate expulsion of his entire family, that he had to leave the door open for us, the younger ones. Thus, every day before dawn, Diogène and Pétion were obliged to accompany him without Papa having been able to oppose it. That took place shortly before the tragedy occurred.

Besides the doubled pay at the end of the week that improved our daily grub, I was the only real beneficiary of my older brothers' work. At night, Pétion was so tired that he didn't act like a foal on a racetrack anymore. After having devoured his portion of the food, he collapsed on the mat like a ripe mango and didn't move any more until Mama came and shook him at the first rustling of a rooster's wings in the vicinity. One sign, however, didn't allow any doubt about the fact that he was alive:

his snoring, a perfect imitation of the whistling of the train that came to pick up the stacks of sugarcane at the plantation's entrance to take them to the factory.

Today, I am neither afraid nor ashamed to say that I was very familiar with that whistling from having had the habit of running behind the train for hundreds and hundreds of meters while Antonio, Hermanos, and some other boys were holding on to it with one hand and throwing stalks of sugarcane to Luciana and me with the other. The group reclining in the grass wasn't long in devouring them voraciously while thanking God for the fact that the commander still hadn't kept the promise he'd made to Papa.

Despite those moments of pure happiness, free of all scholastic constraint, I missed our old life. Indeed, watching, from an elevated position, the wind playing with the cane leaves, it seemed like the ocean's breaking into white caps quivering under the wind's caresses. But it wasn't even an ersatz ocean, like those disgusting concoctions that you pay an arm and a leg for and that don't have the taste or the color or the aroma of coffee. We were surrounded by cane fields. And I missed the ocean, the real one, our ocean, the one that overpowered me, the coming and going of the stevedores stinking with sweat, the sounds of their voices, the lapping of waves against the wharfs, the tossing of those gigantic ropes that had to be grabbed quickly, the prolonged whistling indicating an arrival. In short, everything that accompanied the ship's arrival into port before the descent of the first travelers: the women in crinoline, straw hats, and white gloves, the kids in sailor's collars, all excited, whose parents were always afraid of seeing them tumble into the oily, blackish water, the men wearing linen suits, their handsome looks imbued with everything they had seen over there . . . I had only one wish, and that was to return home, to take up my escapades again, and to undergo the punishments of Mama Lorvanna. My body, like tender grass, was ready to grow back, even if cut to the extreme.

GRANNIE'S STORY

III Three months went by like that, with us frolicking in our carefree existence, thinking our parents had offered us paradise on earth just like chance had offered America to Christopher Columbus. Then tragedy struck. As abruptly as the vigor of a hawk halts the flight of a hummingbird. Accompanied by my two older brothers, Papa arrived early in the afternoon and asked Mama to gather up everything essential: "Round up the kids! We're returning home." He didn't provide her with any further explanation. Perhaps they had already discussed it among themselves.

The efforts of Papa and some boys in the vicinity to find Hermanos, accustomed to wandering far from his home base, were short and unsuccessful. Time was limited. They couldn't prolong their efforts very much without exposing the rest of the family to pointless risks fraught with severe consequences. Only the pounding of fleeing feet and the general panic around us responded to Mama Lorvanna's terror-stricken calls: Helmanooos, Helmanooos. In desperation, Papa had to take her forcefully by the arms and drag her behind him: "We have to go, Nana, let's save those who can be saved." We had just enough time to grab some of our things before throwing ourselves into a veritable manhunt, in which, along with thousands of others, we would constitute, without wanting to, the game to be killed.

Flanked by Papa, leading the march, and by Diogène, who was bringing up the rear, we rushed along the road back without so much as a glance at those places that, for three months, had housed Papa's dreams of El Dorado as well as the carefree life of our childhood. Our steps were jerkier this time. No stops were planned. Neither for water nor for rest. All along the way, Mama wouldn't stop moaning, "My son, my blood, my son, my blood, my son . . ." Followed closely by Pétion, Papa proceeded without saying a word. For his part, Diogène deployed his wealth of tricks to stop the flow of my tears as well as those of Luciana, both of us cognizant by that instinct of women which we weren't yet—scarcely a bud had sprouted on the chest of my elder sister—that a danger was threatening us.

Leaving, there were only the seven members of our family

and several of Papa's colleagues. The more time passed, the bigger the group became: dozens, then hundreds of fugitives came, taking places at our sides, rejoining others ahead. Not even an hour had gone by before we saw clusters of pursued animals, thousands, abandoned in the wilds, without any order or any guide, unprepared for hardship and far from arriving at a safe destination. A long, rough crossing in the dark, riddled with pitfalls, some more hazardous than others, awaited us. While we were fleeing, I could see bloody bodies torn to pieces. They were everywhere, almost as many as those who were still standing, running until their hearts were pounding against their chests. Shots rang out from time to time, drowning out the shouts. Soldiers and men in civilian clothes ran after us, a rifle or a machete in hand, and, having caught up with the slowest, they flailed angrily into the crowd. Sometimes, they worked together to finish off a wounded body, killing it with kicks, rifle butts, machetes, and curses. And my eyes, trying not to miss anything, were fascinated by that morbid attraction hor-ror exercises on us sometimes. One might have said that I was animated by the unflinching intuition that I was going to sur-vive all that, that I needed to capture each detail, to store it in my memory so as to be able to talk about it later, to those who had remained and were dreaming, they too, of leaving. Each time, Diogène would straighten my head in a brutal gesture of protection. And the footsteps that were getting closer to us. The raucous barking of those chasing us was so close that we felt their cold breath breathing down our backs. After several hours of running, we reached a cane field, where they lost our tracks. We had time to rest a bit, for our lungs were on fire, and then continued our flight. Others were less fortunate. I heard one soldier shout: "Mátalo! Mata ese negro maldito!" and another respond to him: "'ta muerto, hombre. 'ta muerto."

I didn't, however, see cane stalks part letting men in from the other direction. Before Luciana and I had time to scream, giant hands clamped our mouths shut. The man who seemed to be the leader ordered Papa to follow him without Papa offering the slightest resistance. Submissive, he followed closely on their heels. That was a shock for me in the midst of so much adversity. I had always thought him capable of flooring five people at the same time. Like Samson. He would only have had to look at them for them to take off with their teeth chattering. But at that moment, no reaction on his part whatsoever. Diogène signaled to Luciana and me not to call out before he positioned himself between us. I didn't feel any anguish in the hand that he held out. It was warm, even serene. That reassured me a bit. Following the three men, the farther we penetrated into the underbrush, the greater our sense of calm. Silent from fear before that, certain people in the group soon rediscovered their use of language, but the leader asked them not to raise their voices. After a half an hour of hurried marching, we arrived at a village where other, more welcoming individuals came to meet us.

We were lodged with the families that met us, their sole recommendation being to not step outside until our rescuers had come to get us. "Unfortunately, you won't be able to stay here for long." We stayed in our hiding place for three days and three nights, attentive to the slightest noise coming from outside. Even the screeching of a cuckoo from the top of a tree found us ready to jump, without any other reflex than that of creating a gap between us and our pursuers. Having understood our anguish, our hosts went so far as to take turns standing guard at night to allow us to recuperate. "You'll need all your strength, amigos. Try to sleep as much as possible." To refuse their offer would have been an insult, but we were unable to close our eyes because our survival instinct was tying our stomachs in knots. During the day, sometimes sleep succeeded in overcoming our resistance and our anguish, but it was brief, agitated, and filled with monstrous nightmares. Those short intervals of dozing off and the copious meals offered by our protectors, however, brought about the renewal of our strength and our optimism. Madame Lorvanna, she didn't eat anything. It was as if she were dazed. Her eyes were distraught, her facial expression absent, and she didn't stop moaning, "My son, my blood, my son . . ." Papa explained to us, to Antonio, Luciana, and me, that we had to return home: "Some nasty people don't want us to stay here, but we shouldn't confuse them with those who sheltered us, even if they are of the same nationality." I have always remembered that phrase each time the urge came over me to amalgamate diverse individuals into one single despicable group.

At the end of that inordinately long wait, our rescuers came to get us. This time, there were five of them, one of whom was armed with a revolver, while the four others were wearing, quite visibly, machetes at their belts. That made Luciana retreat all the way to the back of the house. My father reassured her, and we were able to set off again on the route home. Our anguish, diminished during the wait, was revived as soon as we set foot outside, in spite of our slow pace, feigning confidence to allay suspicion and so as not to attract the attention of possible informers. We accelerated our pace once we got to the underbrush. On the lookout, the five men escorted us. From time to time, one of them shouted something as if to indicate their arrival, a sort of password, for, right afterward, a voice coming from farther away arose: "Sigue! Sigue!" The first moment of fear past, their presence had won the trust of Luciana, who had started to hum so much so that Diogène had to ask her to be quiet. But the silence of my elder sister didn't last long: our guardian angels left us around a dozen kilometers from the border. "We can't accompany you any farther. We have other comrades to pick up, and our network doesn't have enough volunteers. All you have to do is go straight ahead." With a ceremonious gesture, the leader drew his machete from its sheath, gave it to my father, and then gave him a vigorous hug: "Buena suerte, compañero." "Adios, amigo," the others echoed. Not responding, Mama Lorvanna continued to drone, "My son, my blood, my son . . ."

||||||||||||||||||||||||||||||||||||||||||||||||||||||||||||||||||||||||||||||||||||||||||||||||||||||||||||||||||||||||

the sea that one doesn't see that you feel that you imagine rough it bangs with all its weight against the hull the bodies packed in get jammed more it slams they separate it slams bangs she is bad nasty angry vindictive goddess legs and arms entangled head to tail butts crush noses chests mouths stifled cries asphyxia the big boat pitches swells the heart climbs to the mouth exhales in vomiting without end that mixes with the sweat of fear the voices step up the laments evoking marine deities in many languages Yemajá Agwe-Taroyo Loko Papa stop blowing on their animosity reestablish the links of friendship with Agwe links like beads of water the sea that you feel drags the bodies one on top of the other tinkling of chains bodies elevated very high like wisps of defeat and of suffering that fall suddenly allowing the sea to calm down the gods have made peace the bodies end up in their initial spot in the same sausaging some won't move anymore at the next visit of a man from above they'll be thrown overboard.

‖‖‖

IV We had left before dawn in order to avoid the sun that wouldn't have failed to slow us down. If everything went well, when it was at its zenith, we would already be on the other side. At home. Nonetheless, we had to go fast. Very fast. Our steps had resumed their quick pace naturally, still as disorderly for those we were catching up with as for those rejoining us. Except for our little group, which was advancing in stride. When I was tired of trotting in an effort to coordinate my steps with the rhythm of the others, when I would show obvious signs of fatigue, Papa would lift me up off the ground with one hand and fling me over his shoulder, adding a supplemental weight to the enormous sack he already had on his back.

We were advancing with the same sensations we had had three days before. Nothing had changed. Except the ground, strewn with corpses, from which vultures, feeding on them, took off upon our approach before returning to continue their meal. How many hours had passed since our departure? . . . Hermanos had always told me that, as a child, I had eaten the remains of mice. That's how he explained the exceptionally good hearing I demonstrated in circumstances where even a dog, a detector of evil spirits, would have slept soundly.

Speaking of dogs, I was the first to hear their distant yapping, borne by a breeze that caressed our skin early that morning. The same one that I like to feel now touching my neck with its fingers when I warm up like a lizard in the early morning sun. I whispered in Papa's ear that I had heard them, that they were behind us. At other times, he would surely have questioned my word, having always considered me a big storyteller, but then, he asked all of us to accelerate the pace. From a trot, we shifted to a gallop. But the more we advanced, the closer the barking was getting to us. I crossed my fingers furiously until I felt the pain lacerate my bones.

I hoped that perhaps the breeze had played a trick on me. A dirty trick. Like when, the nights of Lent, it enjoyed ushering in, beneath the window of my room, the notes of a *vaksin*. For several minutes, the sound would leave and then return at accordion-like intervals, opening and closing, disappearing for a long minute before reappearing closer to the window, and to my fear. It was there just behind the shutters. The shrill voice of the female singers pierced my eardrums. Their feet slid along the ground in a choreography that I imagined macabre. The *rara* bands, it was said, were not patronized by good Christians. So, I curled up on my bed, looking for refuge under a sheet, too thin in any case, reciting verses that fell from my lips like bullets from a deranged machine gun. A useless screen against the only music that didn't elicit passionate shaking from my body, always ready then to twist itself into contortions at the first drumbeat. Nights like that would drag on as long as days without sun. In the morning, going to see if the nocturnal dancers hadn't left anything buried under the window, I still had the impression that the whole household was making fun of my cowardice.

Unfortunately, it wasn't an auditory illusion. They were really there. Their barking was so close that we crossed a field of ylang-ylangs without me paying attention to it. In other circumstances, I would have had the whole family stop. Then I would have plunged my nose into the intoxicating perfume until I became giddy from it. From that point on, my father ran more than he walked. His feet barely touched the ground. I clung to his shoulder to regulate the bouncing of my head or, at times, to

avoid falling off. Mama Lorvanna was moaning, all the while
eating up the kilometers with the bearing of a marathon runner.
The same for Luciana, her hand in Pétion's. The boys moved
forward with a determined pace as if they knew the route to
take by heart. And the yelping at our heels. Pouring out their
hot breath on our calves. The cries of other groups who'd left
at the same time as us and who will never again hear the sound
of falling rain. The growling of the dogs. The muted sound of
boots. Once again, that injunction embedded in my memory:
"Mátalo!" The ripping of our clothes to escape from brambles,
one of which slashes my face (I still have the scar). With all my
eight years I clench my teeth so as not to scream. So that they
won't find out where I am. Just like I tighten my buttocks so I
won't lose control there on my father's chest. My intestines are
in a vicious struggle with the runs. I can't control my bladder
anymore, which overflows in short bursts. I would suffer from
incontinence for a long time afterward, a habit abandoned when
I started nursery school. And Antonio: "Bed-wetter! Aren't you
ashamed, a big beanpole like you?" He had already forgotten,
Antonio. Or perhaps he didn't see the link to our trip. All the
better for him!

Perched up on Papa's shoulder, I am as out of breath as the
others. My throat is dry like a desert of stones. My chest is on
fire. It would take an entire river to quench my thirst, but I
don't have the time to think about it. The barking. There, right
behind us. Is it the wind or real proximity? I imagine the hounds
fleshy and powerful like horses. They stick their paws on our
backs and tear us apart like my experienced teeth do with stalks
of sugarcane. Just like those that are rising up in front of us, one
pressed tightly against the other, forming a compact field. We
rush in without heeding the leaves. Like sharpened machetes,
their cutting edges dig into our skin. Our bodies are numb to all
pain, other than to the effort deployed in preventing our pursuers from catching up with us.

Just ahead, other groups are trying to escape in the confu-
sion of an army in retreat. Some people can't continue. Lungs
about to explode, they let themselves to fall to the ground, uttering *Ave Marias* and *Our Fathers*. In a sudden silence, a bul-

let pierces the air. The prolongation of the noise in a lingering sound. The running stops for an instant before starting up again in the same chaos. The shock of whining, of tears. Mine and those of Luciana. Those of others as well. The screaming. The barking. Which, later, I would hear all night long, each time I'd close my eyes.

⁣⁣⁣⁣⁣⁣⁣⁣⁣⁣⁣⁣⁣⁣⁣⁣

the waves you don't see them you feel them hear them recede to fill their lungs with water charging at full speed against the hull of the big boat booong they retreat again calm flat as if they had definitively gone cruel illusion booong bong bong bong infernal cadence dozens of them hundreds of them thousands of them assault the big boat shaken like a walnut shell

they don't stop they take turns no respite you imagine them the height of Kilimanjaro banging banging banging filled with resentment toward the boats desecrating the sea's flank this one doesn't even have the time to tilt to one side one two several groundswells stand it up one hits it right in the loins it sways reels several others right it lift it up hold it up in the space between sky and water let it go a shock of an unimaginable violence above the noises of voices orders and counterorders the footsteps of sailors running in all directions the panic of the women crying hysterically the restless dogs baying to the moon their yapping makes you shudder the indifference of the waves that bang bang and bang again

Suddenly, the yapping stopped. Rather, it became distant, almost muffled. If it weren't for the circumstances, one could readily feel as if in a dream. Had we lost our executioners? Had they abandoned the chase? Now that there couldn't be a single one of us left in their country, what else could they want? The explanation wasn't long in coming. We continued to advance with the same resolve. We had to gain more and more ground on them, to not stop until we'd crossed the Massacre River. The more progress we made, with a stride that all the athletes that are talked about so much these days would envy, the hotter we got. The heat was unbearable, inexplicable especially so early in the morning. It had to be eight, nine o'clock. The sun was still hesitating between a caress and a bite. Of course, we provided the effort. Fear was lodged in our stomachs. Our bodies swimming in sweat, a sweat that completely obscured our vision. And that heat . . .

Until we catch sight of the thick smoke that is rising straight up toward the sky. The cane field is in flames. The fire is encircling us. We're caught in the trap. We'll be roasted alive. We're suffocating. A cacophony of sneezes. Some rush out, hands above their heads. The bullets crackle. Crisp salvos accompanied by horrified cries. The wind is blowing, fanning the flames. They roar. Voup! Voooup! Voooup! Delirious onomatopoeia. The sizzling of burning sugarcane. Wounded, some are trying to return to their point of departure. In their eyes, the desire to confront the afterlife in the midst of their own, as if their presence could render the passage easier. But the flames don't allow the realization of their last wish. Incapable of resisting, others leave. The rifles again. Their blasts are followed by a brief silence. As the circle of fire closes up around us, the group gets smaller. Still others attempt a new sortie, in the hope, no doubt, of a better destiny than their predecessors, or a less brutal face-to-face with the other shore.

With the one gallon of water at our disposal, my father has the good idea of dampening bits of cloth, which we wear over our noses in order to breathe. A paltry solution. What protection could Papa invent when, in a couple of minutes, tongues of fire will be licking our arms, our legs, our face? A song surges up from the chest of an old woman. You wonder how she could have run this far. It was picked up in unison by the others. "Closer to you, my God, closer to you . . ." That melody accompanies me often these days. It came like an illumination. I see clearly Shadrach, Meshach, and Abednego in the blazing fire. I forget that behind the curtain of smoke and fire there are dozens of Nebuchadnezzar's soldiers waiting for us, rifle in hand, ready to grab us like ortolans. I close my eyes. I close my eyes. I close my eyes with all the energy of my young age. And I wait.

It was at that moment, when we didn't have any other choice but to confront our destiny, that the rain came. Hard. Violent, even. In vertical sheets mixed with hail. A rain close to a hurricane's, and it wasn't even the season. Some people will surely say that the sky was already overcast and that I hadn't realized it, that it would have been impossible to pay attention to such details given the circumstances. Me, I respond: Evil to whoever doubts the divine mercy of Christ! The shower would last half a day. We took advantage of the first breach that opened in the curtain of fire to set off on a new race. Nothing could stop us, neither the rain that was blinding us nor the mud that was starting to form, making the ground slippery. Antonio, Pétion, and Diogène took turns carrying Luciana, passing her back and forth while they were running. We were no longer very far from our native soil. With a bit of luck . . .

The respite, however, didn't last long. Several hundred yards from the Massacre River, a barrier of armed men, as numerous as the grains of sand from the ocean, was forming. It wasn't enough to stop us. We were determined not to be pushed around anymore. So we charged. A horde of men and women ready to do anything to get to the river, their salvation. Some bodies slump down; the old woman who sang is among them. Trampled, she continues to sing: "Closer to you, my God." Those of our executioners who didn't make way to let us through are crushed. The others resume the attack and the chase. The bullets whistle at our backs. Some of us fall. The most able-bodied pick them up. Others remain on the ground. We have to reach the river. The river. I think that this time my intestines gave way. The dogs again. Their barking. The water in front of us. A few steps away. My vision is getting blurred. Because of the fatigue perhaps. From the sweat and the tears for sure.

I won't hear the dogs—restrained by their masters, preventing them from jumping into the water—yapping with rage. Nor Diogène's screaming when he got hit by a machete on his left leg. I won't see my family cross the river, red with blood, and continue to run even upon entering the town. I won't understand how we were able to reach our old neighborhood along the wharf to start all over again at zero. I'll continue to pretend that Diogène has his two legs and to speak to Hermanos as if he were present.

What have I retained of the language from over there? The eternal question of that rascal Jonas. A few words: "Calao!" the rare times that I get irritated and "'ta buen'" to praise something as a connoisseur, even though I do everything to rid myself of them. I don't remember any others. In school, as was the case for the language of the whites, I refused to study the one from the other side of the mountains in spite of the bad grades I brought home and the scoldings I got for them from Mama Lorvanna: "You'll end up as a fish vendor at the market, you good-for-nothing!" I'll always remember the slap that, many years later, I administered to a young godchild who thought it was clever to respond "sí, señor," "no, señor" to everything said to him. Arnold, go buy me some bread at the store. Sí, señor. Have you brought the wash in already? No, señor. Bam! He never did it again. That language was forbidden in my house. And no longer having the opportunity to address Hermanos to his face, he became "my brother who disappeared" when by chance I had to speak about him to somebody. I decided to refer to Jacques-Antonio as Jacques and Luciana as Luce, in a false affectivity that distanced me from the recurrence of all sounds close to those from over there.

V Since that misadventure, no pitfalls have come upsetting the course of our life. We got our house back, which my parents had had the intuition not to sell. Perhaps they didn't have enough time. In any case, I was extremely happy to see it again. It was as if I were meeting up again with a human being. I wasn't the only one, by the way. Singing and dancing, Luce walked around it three times. Jacques, who never stopped doing silly things, directed a gesture of benediction toward the house. Then he knelt solemnly to kiss the floor of the veranda. Pétion stood him upright with a kick in the buttocks:

"Stop your foolishness, idiot!" In spite of the gravity dictated by the circumstances, my siblings and my parents were hard pressed to hide their joy at returning to their house. No one here would come and confuse them with wild game. I spent several days engaging in light-hearted banter, at a distance, with the ocean, admiring it from the top of the hill, making eyes at it, forever dreaming of crossing it, while, at dusk, the ethereal wind brought its fragrance all the way up to me. Its presence constituted a strong poultice for the wounds brought back from over there.

The trouble with this story was not so much the bitter experience nor the other language over there that made us feel more like foreigners. It was rather staying on the same land. In short, to not really have left. You see, by dint of seeing it there, indifferent like a prison bar, I had ended up believing that all trips necessarily implied the crossing of an ocean. Fording it if necessary. That would have been a way of confronting it, of measuring oneself up against it. The most infuriating thing, I learned later, was that, during the same time period, there were similar possibilities of work on the big island. Boats were the only means of transport to get over there then. Moreover, our people were not received like we were across the border. We lost out on a golden opportunity, one that never presented itself again. Life doesn't offer a second chance, does it? Imagine if we had been on the big island, where the men, they say, are so handsome! I wouldn't have collected those three eyesores with whom I tried to construct my life, and who died on me besides.

Everyone had reimmersed themselves in their routines with incommensurable passion. Papa had no trouble finding a new job, far more gratifying, in fact, than the one before, and he outdid himself in his extravagance for us. It was a still a period when, even without qualifications, you didn't have to go running around in circles for a long time to come up with work. Unless you spent your time dreaming of bringing back, from the bowels of the earth, one of those jars full of gold that the colonists had buried there before leaving. In the hope, of course, of returning to get them. Unfortunately, no man, be he the richest man in the world, is the master of time. Since then, people from here live with the idea of being able to make a fortune without lifting a finger, except perhaps to dig a hole and recover the earthenware jar whose position was revealed to them in a dream.

That's what no doubt explains why Papa dragged us into that affair. All his life, he never stopped looking for the philosopher's stone: in that failed expedition, in inventions for the house, never completed, that were added to a sizeable stack in his dreams that he went over out loud all meal long before our admiring gazes and Mama's half-angry half-flattering one, when it would no doubt have sufficed to look around here. Business wasn't lacking. At least not as much as today. The boats were leaving our shores with their hulls full to the brim, and you saw them lying about on the water like big toads having reveled. Throughout the day, many other boats landed on our shores and vomited a great number of voyagers onto the wharf. Dockers were bustling about like crazy ants; trucks were picking up merchandise to take it who knows where. Construction sites were springing up almost everywhere. There wouldn't be enough able-bodied men for the realization of so many construction projects. Moreover, we saw several Chinese disembark who didn't speak any human language and who, nonetheless, opened the first dry cleaners in the city. Moving directly from the counter of their dry cleaner to that of a restaurant or a bakery, they never slept. They had a business sense disconcerting, to say the least, here where the champions of the siesta were roaming the streets. The Syro-Lebanese, the Jews, and the Palestinians, having arrived poorer than Job, made their fortune and brought their families over.

The police started severely punishing the crime of vagrancy. Every good-for-nothing caught lounging about in the streets without being able to show proof of employment and/or permanent residence was arrested and dragged by force to a construction site where manual labor was needed. One of them, who responded to the name of Masèl Kòkòb, would make life difficult for the policemen, amusing himself for years deriding them. A guitarist from the neighborhood even composed a song in his honor to mock the inability of the police to catch him. But Kòkòb was a victim of his own fame. Even when there was no representative of the forces of order in sight, he couldn't so much as step outside without someone letting out: "Masèl Kòkòb, men chalan dèyè w." And he responding: "Dèyè papa w!" In the end, as soon as he heard, or thought he heard, even the whistling of the air, he got edgy. And, by imagining responses to stave off attacks from grown-ups and kids, he went crazy, stark-raving mad when the song was taken up by a carnival band that popularized it throughout the entire city. That day, we barely avoided a tragedy: Masèl Kòkòb, who had threaded his way through the crowd around the procession, threw a stone at the head of the singer, who almost fell from the top of the float but was caught by a musician just in time. The police took advantage of the incident to seize the man and to lock him up in a psychiatric ward. We never heard anything else about him.

Except for that incident, time passed in a peaceful manner, smoothly and quietly. Mama Lorvanna had gotten her dress-maker's table back, for domestic use, and her manual sewing machine. Her clients returned as if she had never left the neighborhood or had just gone on vacation. And things were vigorously discussed: a price deemed too high was lowered, the request, for the following day, of a dress for a wedding, a burial or a first communion: "You know, my dear, money doesn't always come when we want it to." And Mama would measure, cut, sew, let the scraps fall to the ground, which filled me with joy, more so than Luce and Vénus, my younger sister, the last born of the family. She's the proof, if there was any need for it, that my parents hadn't lost all sense of pleasure. But, from time to time, when Mama was supposed to be working, one of us would surprise her, her eyes staring blankly into space with two streams of tears running silently down the length of her cheeks and her lips muttering inaudibly: "My son, by blood, my son . . ." Lamentations we would hear for the rest of our lives.

Until her death, which occurred when she was over ninety-six years old, Mama refused to face the facts, and saved money, penny by penny, to finance searches over there with the idea of finding Jacques's twin brother. She didn't want us to say a mass for the eternal rest of his soul, either, in spite of Papa's insistence. One day he got angry and decided to not talk about it anymore. "That would be," she would say, "like renouncing the idea of seeing him alive again. As long as there is a chance of that, I will continue to fight. I will only admit defeat when I read his duly authenticated death certificate." What had happened to our brother? Had they caught him, too, and thrown him in a common grave? Had he been devoured by their huge hounds? Had he been welcomed by a family that, since no one had come to claim him and since his skin was rather light so as not to give rise to any doubts about his origin, had finally adopted him? Often, while I was watching the boats and letting, as usual, my imagination drift without being aware of it, I would vanish into my dreams. Just like Hermanos had prophesied.

||||||||||||||||||||||||||||||||||||||||||||||||||||||||||||||||||||||||||||||||||||||||||||||||||||||||||||||||||||||||||

a song arises from time to time a capella from a voice you thought extinguished grave sad of a sadness that only concerns itself tremor of fatalism the voice is transformed into a chant in rhythm with the lapping of the waves against the hull of the big boat it invades steerage drowned in its sepulchral silence pierces the shadows the others sleep dreaming perhaps of the time that was but not the voice perpetuated in other voices the chant fills the hold of the big boat explodes invades the bridge mingles with the wind the sails swollen to the point of breaking oh stele

and the ship advances pushed by all those voices down in the hold

sudden headache a human on the bridge can't take it anymore tired of those animal chants the raised hatch filters through the voice of other animals the yelping of dogs that are located above in cages of wire mesh apocalyptic barking like the rumbling of thousands of thunderbolts the sky that collapses the voices cut off abruptly as they had started letting the silence and the shadows regain possession of steerage permeated only by the tempo of the waves

||||||||||||||||||||||||||||||||||||||||||||||||||||||||||||||||||||||||||||||||||||||||||||||||||||||||||||||||||||||||||

VI We had to learn to live in the absence of a family member, something that we others, sisters and brothers, succeeded in rather well. Jacques became a professor, to the great displeasure of Papa, who was already seeing him as a doctor sounding the chests of the injured and the rejects of the neighborhood for free. Besides being a dreamer, Papa also had the soul of a Good Samaritan, which made Mama say: "The day when we won't have anything to feed our children, I hope that your beggars will hold out their wooden bowls under the porch of the cathedral and return to you, in that way, a bit of what you have given them." It's not that Mama Lorvanna was stingy, nor that she had a heart of stone, but she always saw to it that we were never lacking anything at home. In any case, it would have been difficult for Jacques to become a doctor. At that time, being able to wear a white coat was a big deal, a privilege that families far more classy than ours had made their private hunting preserve. Jacques, who wasn't patient, went directly into teaching before going into business for himself several years later and opening a superb five-story school.

As for Diogène, he had never liked sitting on the benches at school. He eventually decided to make them for the buttocks of others, hiring and firing, one after the other, apprentices he spent his time arguing with. A good guy in spite of his surly side, he was the first to offer them a helping hand as soon as one of them found himself in financial straits: an impromptu birth, a baptism, a grave sickness. Then he would propose a loan that would never be paid back or offer a job more fictitious than real even when his shop was virtually running in neutral. Because of that, he lost his wife, who didn't have the patience of Mama Lorvanna with Papa and disappeared, leaving him with their only son on his hands. He didn't change, for all that, and turned into a cantankerous old bachelor.

Becoming a foreman on a construction site that the whites had opened in the South before their departure, Pétion was the first one to leave the family shell. Once a month, he would come to see us at the wheel of an enormous dump truck into which he tried, in vain, to hoist Mama Lorvanna. I don't know what he was up to down there, but, after his death, not a year went by without a young man or a young girl presenting his- or herself to the family as being born of his work. It would have been bad form on our part to deny the fact, for those children of sin were often his spitting image. His widow—one couldn't have been more indulgent—would take them in for a year or two, in a large house that the deceased had constructed outside of town, until one day they decided by themselves to return to where they came from, without giving any further sign of life.

As for Luce, in spite of her bad character, which had distanced more than one interesting suitor, she was successful in finding a husband who watered down her wine and gave her five brats to raise just as recalcitrant as their mother. Since the drubbings never stopped, the children often chose to take asylum at my house. Luce would then accuse me of being too lenient with them and called me a fence. I wasn't going to spoil her children. All I had to do was give birth to others (I had had one boy), if my uterus hadn't become sterile from having done forbidden things. Those accusations didn't help improve a relationship that has always been tense between us since childhood. Vénus, she married a butcher whose true name, up until the moment I am speaking now, I have never known. Everyone called him Condor, a name that, hearing it, has no human sound, don't you agree? What would irritate me the most was when people, super-serious, would appear in front of the veranda: "Is Mrs. Condor there, if you please?" "—Someone told you that such a person lives here?" I'll give you the names with which I rewarded the intruder, who would withdraw faster than he had arrived. My curses, which can crack like a whip, followed him until he disappeared from my sight.

Do I have to elaborate on my rather turbulent married life? Two marriages, one cohabitation, and three burials, which I could have easily done without. Like, I might add, the insinuations of the gossips, according to whom I had sold my soul, already damned by men, to the devil to get rich. Admittedly, one of them left me a small inheritance that I added to the savings of Jonas's parents to buy the house we live in now. That's it. If not, I would not have taken up a profession as uncertain as Mama's

THE OTHER SIDE OF THE SEA

after having stopped my studies one year before getting my elementary school certificate: my health, rather shaky, didn't allow me to go any further. After all, my generation didn't go to school as walk-on extras; we learned something there. One can't say that is the case these days. When I hear the children of the neighborhood mutilate a beautiful language like French, not only do I feel sick, but I also ask myself if it's worth it to spend so much money to teach them such stupidities. They might as well become porters right away. And those things are said in rhetoric or philosophy class! . . . Let's return to my impossible loves with men before I get carried away.

If I am grateful to a man, it's to my first husband. I am indebted to him, in a certain sense, for a descendent that doesn't resemble him. That Jonas's father didn't come out similarly shaped, like the bear of the fable, that is a miracle pure and simple. It's as if nature had fun making him the exact opposite of his progenitor. I could have, of course, chosen someone less close to an ape, but handsome men have this in common with the ocean: they think you are always at their disposition. Except for that little debt, I have never agreed to play the role of a ripe banana for a decayed tooth, like those women who get slapped and retreat into a corner to cry, waiting for their torturer to come and console them. In that regard, I am conscious of not having followed the precepts of Christ to the letter. Besides, what man would have dared raise his hand to my face? It wouldn't be long before I'd be running into him, headfirst, and throwing at his face everything that came into my hands: hairbrush, bottles, mirror, plates, glasses . . . everything. Then I would throw all his things out on the street. With a broom, off with you! My fights with my second husband were the talk of the town. They were veritable battles of titans. My third try, I straight out rejected marriage, preferring to live in sin rather than suffer the yoke of a man. It would be easier to get rid of him when the time came, I said to myself. All the more so since I had decided to live under my own roof. The poor sergeant didn't give me the opportunity . . . But enough. Let's put aside those stories of men I don't have anything to do with anymore:

39

GRANNIE'S STORY

I have already explored the question from all angles and arrived
at a true sense of peace.

||||||||||||||||||||||||||||||||||||||||||||||||||||||||||||||||||||||||||||||||||||||||||||||||||||||||||||||||||||

now the big boat is gliding over a calm sea nothing is trou-
bling sleep in the darkness of steerage neither the noise of the
wind in the sails nor the curved swells of the backwash that
come indicating the exertion of the prow cleaving its way
through the aquatic mass on the bridge no longer any noise
of steps bringing nightmares to sleep except the trip toward
the beyond the knowledge of the world the boat is sinking the
waves have disappeared left to rest from their efforts in the
bowels of the marine immensity harassing other boats toward
other shores and the livestock is sleeping dreaming of the shores
left behind of initiation rites to life of dances with levitation
around the fire tracking prey in the heart of the forest contact
of hands on hard breasts amidst the clanking of chains the livestock sleeps while the big boat continues its journey toward the
unknown it dreams that it never wakes up

||||||||||||||||||||||||||||||||||||||||||||||||||||||||||||||||||||||||||||||||||||||||||||||||||||||||||||||||||||

VII

For some as well as for others, their time had been
spent in a city prone to expansion despite the
ocean. Sometimes, I would come across faces that
I couldn't identify, whose history and ancestry I wasn't familiar with. The number was diminishing, from day to day, of
those whom one could ask, at the corner of the street, for news
about their family. And the kids? And your health? Did your
little one successfully complete his certificate? Faced with this
new phenomenon, I clung to the branches—there were quite a
few—of the family tree. Except for Pétion, who, in any case,
had set himself up on the town's periphery, we were all living in the neighborhood of my childhood, and there was no
lack of reasons to meet. Nor things to talk about. At no point,
however, did we speak about the thing among ourselves. It was

as if Diogène had always gone through life on a wooden leg, and, above all, we didn't listen to the lamentations of Mama Lorvanna. Life had reasserted itself, with its procession of responsibilities, of joys, of new sorrows, and, more than halfway through, the journey, which Mama would complain about all day long, didn't seem that difficult: "Ala pasay!" Her long sighs seemed to come from the tips of her toes and to have traveled through her entire body before being exhaled in the form of an interminable moan. Henceforth, with her aging accelerating, the premature death of Papa, and, with the possible exception of Jacques, who gave the impression of not having been vaccinated against such a preposterous idea, only the Great Trip caused any anxiety to some among us.

It was during this period—Papa's body hadn't yet gone cold— when the calamity, which came from the most distant part of the ocean, swept down upon our city. Hitting the vital forces of our population, it would spread like an epidemic. Doctors, nurses, teachers, agronomists . . . were its main victims. They threw themselves headfirst into the undertaking as if it were a war. Job offers with truly enticing terms came in by the thousands. Few managers here were in a position to refuse them. They responded en masse, all the more so since, after many vicissitudes, we had entered a new period of lean times. From there to so frenziedly cutting the umbilical cord . . .

Now that you can throw stones without hiding your hand, I mean without fear of disappearing in broad daylight, there is no longer any reason to be quiet. It seems quite strange to me, by the way. Only yesterday, you were mistrustful of your neighbor, your servant, your spouse, of one's own blood: prudent, not a coward, right? Truth be told, all those people who left, or who dreamed of doing so, were not hit with mass insanity, even if that seemed to be the case.

Everything had started before anyone realized it. Not even Antoine Langommier, although he was used to warning us in time about dangers that loomed over the city with their talons deployed. Thus, the population had succeeded in nipping them in the bud. But this time, the thing had advanced secretly, had swollen progressively and then taken on such a vastness that everyone had ended up depending on the caprices of a single man. Cerberus would voluntarily compare himself to God and let it be understood that his reign over the city was going to last a thousand years. During that time, either you toed the line or his thugs would turn you into a diversion to beat the heat. Many pregnant women, simply from having looked at his picture, had a miscarriage at that very minute or gave birth to a little monster with twelve fingers and other strange things.

That proposition, coming from the other side of the ocean, allowed the city's new master to get rid of some of the unruly and some of the hotheads without opposition. All those who were out of favor with the authorities, first and foremost the professors, were warmly invited to take advantage of the offer. The rapidity of the invitation varied in relation to the jealousy aroused. A house for which you had been offered a laughable price, without, moreover, its having been put up for sale, and that you had had the audacity to refuse. A wife whose beauty had attracted the desire of one of the regime's henchmen. Lacking the necessary qualifications to apply to leave the country, you found yourself bound hand and foot in a prison cell, accused of conspiring against the state security. In the best of cases, the detention would last until your wife, after having knocked at all the doors, agrees, in desperation, to pay the price of your liberation. If the ape was really stuck on her, it was exile or your disappearance. The ugly women became quite prosperous and highly respected during that time; they became housewives of men for whom they wouldn't even have served as backups during a night of want. As a consequence, one of them proposed to her colleagues the creation of a "Committee in Support of Women in Action for the Perpetuity of the Regime."

However, amidst the reported-missing, the sent-packing-according-to-the-wise-suggestions-of-parents-or-friends, the thrown-one-night-into-an-airplane-without-the-time-to-change-or-to-say-goodbye-to-the-family, the hemorrhage got worse, while those in power were worried about their reputation beyond the borders of the city. Henceforth, all managers who hadn't received the authorities' authorization were forbidden to leave our shores. Thus, the "fugitives" were arrested at the airport and at border crossings and forcibly brought back to their family after having received a severe beating. It was forbidden to look at an airplane, or a boat, too intently. Every person who requested a passport was put on file, registered, as well as numbered, and could be the object of a strong-arm police inquiry at any hour of the day or night. Vendors of false travel documents proliferated like shit on the butt of a mare. Often, they were spies for those in power and, instead of a passport, the client would receive a dissuasive beating. In the end, when that happened, he was only too happy not to have lost anything other than some money . . .

||||||||||||||||||||||||||||||||||||||||||||||||||||||||||||||||||||||||||||||||||||||||||||||||||||||||||||||||||||||

the big boat is reeling under the added weight of the chant heels measuring the pain against the hull broken syncopated voices rhythmic chorus colliding with fragments of darkness up above is it night or day the fervor of voices baritoning from the deepest domain of suffering exploding on the surface of being without the hand gesture of any chorus leader

from time to time the clamor recedes except a melodious hum floating in the air hummed from the hollow of the throat stops and then starts again unless it has never really stopped

||||||||||||||||||||||||||||||||||||||||||||||||||||||||||||||||||||||||||||||||||||||||||||||||||||||||||||||||||||||

This is when my son, he, too, contemplated leaving. At a time when, except for the limited—when all is said and done—experience of Pétion, no member of the family should have been contemplating such an eventuality. Until that pipe dream, though, he hadn't shown any symptoms of the desire to move. He wasn't part of that group of men who take their house for a hotel-restaurant, only entering to eat, sleep, and yell at wife and kids. He always left with a precise destination: to go to work, to visit his fiancée, a splendid young woman whom I liked very much and who returned my affection one hundred times over. Thus, the news had the effect on me of a parasitic plant that, from one day to the next, you see growing in your garden. I didn't let my anger show on the spot, but if someone had been able to open my veins, they wouldn't have found the slightest drop of blood.

However, I was not disposed to keep that serpent in my breast. I've always said, "While I am alive, nobody from my family will leave the shores of this city." So that all of this remains somewhat inhabited and doesn't become a wasteland haunted only by the words of the wind, the fury of the sun, and the memory of those who once lived here. At the rate things were going, my fears were more than justified. Moreover, it wasn't just next door: one had to swallow some ocean to get there. To be sure, we are a people who have traveled a lot, but really . . . How would I have been able to visit my son when I wanted? Incidentally, except for the color of our skin, we haven't had anything to do with those people since the old tribal struggles of Guinea. Of course, some people here continue beating, like maniacs, the drum of their pagan religion, preventing honest people from sleeping the sleep of the righteous. But me, I've never wanted to hear anything about those practices which weren't decreed by Our Lord. When was this thing revealed? Where is the sacred writing that validates it? For my part, I'm sticking to the commandments in the Bible.

Thus, it was out of the question that my son go to that out-of-the-way country where he wouldn't even know the goat grazing at the foot of a baobab. And besides, even if they had called you, that doesn't mean that later they wouldn't give you a kick in the rear. There was a time when the people from the other side of the mountains came here themselves to look, even into our nooks and crannies, for our compatriots. They promised them a fortune, jewels that they had never seen nor dared to imagine, the earth and the sky combined. Some listened and sold their small houses, their patch of land, thinking they were leaving forever. In any case, if they returned, they would stay in luxury hotels, where they would be received like Arabian princes. Instead of that, bullets, the blows of machetes. Dogs with raucous voices. And their return in spite of themselves: one hand in front, one behind.

No one is waiting for you in a foreign land. How do you

explain that to someone as stubborn as a mule? And since he was teaching in secondary school, he was certainly not far from thinking that he knew more about life than me. To see his crazy enterprise through, he allied himself with Jacques, who, since his most tender infancy, exercised a bad influence on him. Moreover, it's because of his imitating Jacques that he had taken up teaching.

Suspecting my reaction, Jacques had taken the initiative, selecting, for that matter, a very bad moment: I had to deliver an urgent order. And that day, I wasn't in the mood to chat. Nonetheless, he tried to explain to me the wonderful opportunity that my son was presented with: "I myself, had I been a bit younger, I would have jumped at the chance." "It's never too late to be an idiot," I retorted. Thinking he was pleasing me, he added, "There are opportunities that you can't miss. A missed chance doesn't return, Noubòt." Just to remind me of our old complicity. An emphatic stare on my part was enough to send him on his way, his tail between his legs. Having arrived near the fence, he nonetheless let out, "He's no longer a child, you know." As if I didn't know that myself and I hadn't seen him grow like a beanpole.

Hence the difficulty in forbidding the trip straight out, as if he were an adolescent with only fuzz on his chin. I had to bring him around to renouncing his trip without ruffling his male sensibility. Oh, you can't imagine how complicated men are, and fragile above all. But I didn't have to think about it for long. I had the solution within arm's reach, so to speak. One afternoon when he wasn't home, his fiancée visited me, as was her habit, through my impetus to tell you the truth. She was a bit like the daughter I would have liked to have had. Without even giving her the time to greet me or to sit down, I attacked, asking her what they were waiting for to set up a household. "You know, a woman has a clock somewhere inside that registers the ticks. If you don't hear them, afterward it's too late. Not to mention the fact that another woman, shrewder, can always steal him from you. A man, I told her, is like corn that you put out to dry in the sun. You planted it, watered it, protected it from the pelicans, picked it, shucked it, winnowed it, spread it out patiently over the esplanade, turned it over from time to time so that it didn't burn, brought it in when it was threatening to rain, and you would let any chick coming from who knows where come in here and eat it, reap the rewards of your own labor."

Gradually, as I developed my argument, I saw panic overtaking her. Her face was transformed before my very eyes. It lost that reserved facade that she would always adopt in my presence and became that of a tigress, ready to do anything to defend her prey. I smiled to myself and pounded the nail in. "How much time have you been going out together?" "Three years, mamie." "Three years! That's an investment, my dear. And if he were to abruptly decide to go abroad? These days a frenzy of departure is spreading over the city. He, too, could be smitten with it. You never know. And would you let him go like that, waiting until he returns to marry you? At your age, you still believe in Santa Claus. Not even a month would go by before you wouldn't have any more news from him. We're the only ones who allow our men to do whatever they want. Foreign women, they don't joke around . . . You are a woman, aren't you? I don't have to draw a picture for you. Besides, I have been dreaming of a grandson for a long time. I would call him Jonas." I goaded her to the hilt that day. A month later, she came, all smiles, to announce that she had a beautiful illness. All I had to do was ask my son to accept his responsibilities. I wasn't about to back his banditry. In less time than it takes to say it, he found himself before the registrar. All the family and a good part of the neighborhood came to enjoy themselves at their wedding.

That feminine coalition was, however, far from sufficient. Some people, when they've gotten an idea into their head, the earth can wobble on its pedestal, even collapse, and they won't budge. It's like tortoises, which seem so harmless, quick to retract their heads under their shells at the slightest noise, but beware of their bite! As long as a she-ass has not brayed seven times, they won't let go. And you still have to find an ass and make it bray. My son was of that race, and I am very much afraid that my little Jonas has inherited that character trait. To make a long story short, what I thought was the supreme obstacle turned out to be simply an annoying delay that schemes slightly more elaborate were able to circumvent, for, once their file is accepted, applicants could leave the country with the members of their family. Nothing prevented my daughter-in-law, my ally for an afternoon, from shifting into the opposing camp. Life teems with spectacular reversals like that. Her marital bliss was at stake. And, at two against one, I hadn't yet won the battle.

VIII

Despite my efforts, which dragged on forever, my stupid ass of a son wouldn't budge from his idea of traveling, until the day the beast made its mark on one of us. Even if you know that you have to keep your beard drenched when your neighbor's is on fire, you don't feel the matter concerns you as long as the flames aren't at your door . . .

The son of Vénus had married a nurse, she, too, attracted by the sirens that were coming from the other shore. No voice, not even that of reason, could have stopped her. She was already picturing herself as having a nice home with her husband and two or three kids who would speak only the gibberish of over there. In fact, she succeeded in leaving, but at night, disguised as a nun. Sacrilegious, don't you think? Think a bit about the anguish that was wracking the guts of those close to her. What if she were recognized! Vénus fainted when two men knocked at her door telling her that her daughter-in-law had arrived on the other side without any problem. She thought that they had come to inform her of her arrest. She already saw a battalion of those bastards turning up to interrogate the members of her family one by one, destroy, room by room, the house that the Condor had bequeathed to her. When she learned that her eldest daughter and her husband, a lawyer by profession, had also defied the ban on travel and were on foreign soil—they hadn't informed her for fear of worrying her—her heart, which was fragile, gave out.

Consequently, what should have been a moment of rejoicing ended up being a long procession—she had always known how to pamper the people of the neighborhood—behind a hearse one afternoon when even the dull blue-green water of the docks stopped its swirling to watch her pass by for the last time. Two men had to support Mama Lorvanna, already rather old, who was reviling God with heart-rending insults for taking away the beings dearest to her: "Are you going to eat all of them? Will you never have enough of them? Where is your mercy? Why don't you take me, me, too?" But in his magnanimity God surely shouldn't pay attention to the diatribes of a soul in pain.

In the meantime, it was André's, the only son of Diogène, turn to want to follow in the tracks of his cousins. His father had, though, forbidden it in his way, which is to say harshly and awkwardly. The discussion couldn't have been more stormy that day. It ended with the throwing of a crutch at André's head, the same one that Diogène had made so as not to have to use the artificial limb that had been fitted for him at the hospital where his leg was amputated. He growled with his cavernous voice—he groused all the time that he didn't give a damn about a false limb, that it wouldn't return the leg to him that those idiot doctors hadn't known how to treat. If it hadn't been for the presence of Mama, he would have thrown the crutch at one of them: "I wonder if one day they won't send back to us all those who left, because over there, it's not like here. If you treat a sick person badly, they slap a trial on your ass and throw you in the clink." I don't know where he had dug up those lies and especially that vulgarity. Nonetheless, when he wanted to shine at a special occasion, he put up perfectly well with his artificial limb. Of course, he limped badly, but that wasn't due to his wooden leg: he had always limped.

To return to the discussion between father and son, it was a miracle that the crutch didn't poke André's eye out that day. Having lost his equilibrium, Diogène found himself with his ass on the ground, uttering the worst curses, accompanied by severe threats directed at his only son. "If you leave, you will no longer have a father. Keep that in mind. I'm giving you until noon tomorrow to come to be forgiven." André, who was already a man, didn't return the next night. Who knows what dive he hung out in. Quite taken with the men from here, the girls from the other side of the mountains had already started crossing the border, bringing loose morals to the bars of the port. Already when he was young, André was fond of both the thing and the bottle, activities he never succeeded in dragging my son into in spite of his desire. The next day, he had already forgotten the maledictions of his father when the clock of the basilica reminded him of them by ringing out midday's twelve chimes. André took to his heels, saying to himself that he had no reason to have a falling out with the old man, as he called him, especially at such an important moment.

Having arrived home, he entered without knocking, beaming, just to let the old man think that everything was forgotten, that it had only been a passing incident like those that occur in the best families. He saw Diogène stretched out on the bed, his arms crossed over his chest. He wondered about the fact that someone as indefatigable as his father wasn't in his workshop planing, sawing, and polishing with all his might. André called out to him, remaining all the while right next to the door, thus able to leap outside in case the old man were, as was his habit, to play a trick on him and grab him by the collar and beat him black and blue with a small leather strap he had baptized B12. For Diogène, there was no fixed age for manhood: "He will be an adult the day he's not under my roof anymore, and even then . . ." André called out a second time, then a third even louder, until the whole neighborhood rushed into the house. He had just lost his father, whose body, still warm, was carried with great difficulty to the morgue by all those who had benefited from his generosity.

No one knew the real causes of Diogène's death. Some evoked the failure of his workshop, which was operating only because of his stubbornness. Others spoke of his nostalgia for the night, during which he loved to go all over the place, dialoguing at times with the phantoms of the city, at others with his own shadow, until he collapsed from fatigue and lack of sleep. No one ever alluded to any responsibility whatsoever of André's in the affair. Everyone found it quite natural that he'd thought about looking for greener pastures, heading for other shores. All the more so since clouds, laden with a thousand forms of present and future pain, were continuing to accumulate.

There was no wake. They had recently been forbidden by the new master of the city. Wakes, which continued very late into the night, gave rise to too many tears and, at the same time, to too much rejoicing. A comingling that was difficult to control. In fact, the night belonged to his henchmen, released like vultures on the city's fear. The funeral was of a rare solemnity in the neighborhood. The faces were dignified and grave, except that of Mama Lorvanna, who no longer had the strength to cry or to follow the hearse and had been put in a car. André wasn't long in leaving, he, too, for the other side of the water. We only heard tell of him when he wanted us to.

||||||||||||||||||||||||||||||||||||||||||||||||||||||||||||||||||||||||||||||||||||||||||||||||||||||||||||||||||||||||||||||

in the night in steerage bodies seek out each other resist each other brief struggle and without pity of animals at bay honor to the victors groans short and rapid indifferent look of the vanquished final panting then the decycled sleep for some others eyes open in the darkness penetrating the memory of the time that was hundreds of distinct snores clash responding to the crashing of the waves against the hull of the big boat fending its way from nowhere to an elsewhere heavier than time

||||||||||||||||||||||||||||||||||||||||||||||||||||||||||||||||||||||||||||||||||||||||||||||||||||||||||||||||||||||||||||||

Without saying a word, my son was present at those departures. The summons still not having come—to my great pleasure, though mitigated by the unbearable tension generated by the wait—I would carefully avoid talking to him about it so as not to throw oil on the fire. Anyway, it wouldn't have helped. He would have taken refuge in silence, cutting short, in that way, every attempt at discussion. But I sensed his conviction was wavering. Not enough, however, to make him abandon the idea. And if the invitation had arrived during that period, he would have distanced himself from his native land without regrets, so much did he seem revolted by the turn of events.

The entire city was living withdrawn into itself, in a fear until then unknown. Formerly so beautiful, the night of the city belonged from then on to silence, one punctuated from time to time by calls for help from a mother, a female companion, a brother whom everyone pretended not to hear. Tongues seemed cast in lead while individual disappearances took place at vespers.

I was losing hope of finding a way to convince my son to give up his idea when Jonas was born. The little scoundrel had shown up with his two feet first, and it wasn't a minor affair to get him out of there (there is no point insisting on the price his coming into the world cost his parents, who were obliged to sell their house to pay for the services of a young specialist newly graduated from German universities). The obstetrician had to be helped by a nurse in pulling like a maniac; each one was holding a leg that slipped out of their hands because it was so slimy.

When I saw him, I immediately knew that it was going to be a devil of a job to keep him here. If, at the end of only seven months, he had felt cramped in there, what would happen when he started to evolve in this city shriveled up like an old mango, overwhelmed by the heat, the dirt, and malicious gossip? Already, he had that smile, a bit ironic, on his lips of someone prepared to confront both the light and the darkness of the world at the same time. But we were really meant for each other, he and I. If necessary, I was prepared to tie him to the leg of a table to rid him of his desire to sneak off and go wandering about all day long when he got big, he, too, attracted by the lures from the other side of the waters.

Truth be told, except for his little jaunts in the vicinity, he has never given me reason to complain. He even seems to be bound to this patch of earth like a shipwrecked man to a lifeline. That doesn't prevent me from calling him "Powdered Feet," so that, even while joking, he doesn't forget where his moorings are. It's like the bells that you hear ringing over there on the other side of the mountains. The timbre that gets to us is so pure—rid of all scoria, without anything that aggresses the ear—that we imagine them different and above all more beautiful than the ones here. And the bell tower that houses them. The chapel. The ground where the chapel was erected. And our imagination is liberated, without any bridle to curb its surge. We burn with desire to go see it. Which is natural, after all. The trouble is that you can find yourself caught in your own trap. It's like the mouse that's gone too close to the bait. One time is enough, you know, and you don't find your way back. Our parents had told us that we were going to spend a bit of time over there, and it lasted three long months.

Often, I think about all those incidents, about the events that followed, and I say to myself: God has honored me like no other in giving me a grandson like Jonas. If not, what sense would my life have had? For whom would I have worked so much, to the point of becoming disabled from it? An individual is above all a family, and that family holds together for the most part in one's memory . . . When his heart moves him, my little Jonas and I spend hours talking about everything and nothing. About his faith, which he doesn't like to talk about too much even though he did his schooling at a religious school. (I moved heaven and earth for him to be enrolled in that school. If not, what would his adult life have been based on?) I share secrets with him. I don't have anything to hide anymore, do I? When it seems to me that he's not disposed, I talk to myself, or to the wind. But my words are far from being empty chatter: sooner or later the wind will return and recount them to him. And since I often see him bent over a sheet of paper with a pencil in his hand, I hope he will make a story with them in his fashion, that he will share it with the other members of the human family. Thus, all that won't have been in vain. I won't read that story, I, who have always loved poking my nose into books (that keeps the brain active). That's not so bad. For my part, the ideal would be, upon my departure from life, that my coffin be cast off onto the waves and that I'm allowed to drift to my eternal rest. The time for me, with a quick glance over to the other side, to know if the reality corresponded to my dreams. Oh, afterward, I'd return to rest among the members of my family, for what is the value of such an experience if you can't come back and recount it to those who stayed? See their eyes stare wide open with emotion, look at you like a ghost that had rubbed shoulders with the afterlife. But all that's nothing but idle fancy. I know that no one will accede to my wishes (the caprices of an old woman, they will say), not even my little Jonas.

IX A long time later, when I had had to move to another neighborhood, the boats were already no longer used for anything except to transport merchandise and people who were leaving on cruises, or who were coming from nowhere, filled with tourists ready to marvel at the slightest trinket. In any case, my steps had trouble making it to the wharf's guardrails, where the passers-by, seeing me deeply absorbed in the contemplation of the ships, took me for an old-fashioned romantic, a deranged woman hoping for the return of a lover who'd left light years ago. It's not only in books and at the movies that one sees such fables. And as it's been ages since I've cared anything about those stories involving men, it's better to stay in one's place, isn't it?

By a stroke of good fortune, the new house that I'm still living in with Jonas is located right next to the airport that serves domestic flights. Formerly, early in the morning, using the pretext of going to get some sun, I would spend hours watching the airplanes come to warm up at the end of the runway before taking off in a noise of steel, carrying away my stare and my imagination. For, in spite of it, in spite of the time that had elapsed, I hadn't completely rid myself of my dreams of elsewhere. Like a toy that you play with endlessly. And I would watch those monsters elevate into the air, raise their crests, proud like roosters after making love, turn over on their right wing feigning a spin, then straighten up nimbly to lose themselves in the clouds.

But despite the prowess they demonstrated in flying and in not falling again after takeoff, in my mind, they hadn't replaced the boats, which have that capacity to take up the rhythm of the waters in order to advance, sometimes even against their furor. Perhaps the air doesn't have the same effect on me as the liquid immensity. And if I, too, had had to leave, I would have chosen a boat, partly so as not to distance myself all at once from my city. All things considered, the only times those machines succeeded in extracting a cry of admiration from me was when they would pirouette above the ocean, go into a nosedive as if they were going to plunge into the ocean for good before elevating their steel frames and setting off again straight ahead. Imagine one of them, would to God that it doesn't, crashing into the water with all those people inside and the windows closed. What an atrocious death that would be!

After those acrobatics, I could stay for hours, my eyes riveted on the horizon—if I didn't have to finish a dress for a demanding client, of course—trying to relate the idle fancies of an old lady to those of my youth. Until Jonas, the little snoop, pops up and calls out to me, "Grannie, what are you dreaming about yet again?"

What do I say to him? That I'm trying to reassemble my dreams and my recollections, which, henceforth, form only one single, faded bouquet? That it's way too late to cross the ocean? My legs, those pillars of Hercules, don't support me anymore. I wouldn't take two steps before I'd collapse. In any case, I don't want to anymore. My heart isn't in it. With the passing of time, I've seen so many people leave. Very few have returned to their point of departure. Those who've tried weren't long in rediscovering the mystery left back there. Who has seen water return to its source before? Today, people leave earlier and earlier. The neighborhood is losing its young people like a necklace its pearls. And me, I'm staying here, guardian of a temple whose walls, because of their cracking, will end up collapsing. Like me disappearing into my dreams. I'm still waiting for my brother's prediction to come true for good. And when I stare at the horizon like that, I'm only trying to recall the name, the face, the voice, the gait, and sometimes the history of those who have gone. They have been or are (are they still living?) the pages, the unfinished chapters, even, of my life. Who will remember them when I'm no longer here?

THE OTHER SIDE OF THE SEA

Recently, it's as if a virus had swept down on the city hitting families in turn, not sparing even the most well-off. Not a month goes by, not even a week, without someone, their face misty with bittersweet tears, coming up and greeting me: "God has listened to our prayers, Grandmother. The departure is set for this afternoon." For him and for those close to him, even for his enemies, with whom he is gladly reconciled the day of his departure, leaving is always good news, even if he is unaware of what is waiting for him over there. Oh, his happiness is not difficult to understand when you've seen him hang out on the sidewalk the whole blessed day trying to kill time, which refuses to die. I have watched all the young people grow up as if they had been my own grandsons! I spend entire days holding back my tears, wishing good luck, my son, good luck, my daughter! I will pray for you. May God guide your steps in the unknown snow! And I shake their hands or I embrace them. That's according to the degree of intimacy that connects us.

How does one swim against the current and play the kill-joy? Except, of course, when it's a question of an older man or an older woman, who has already bought and sold everything life had to offer, and turns up in front of you, dolled up like a first communion cake, twiddling her thumbs without knowing where to start and ends up confessing to you: "I'm going to see my daughter, neighbor. Don't you remember her? The one who got married to a citizen over there. I showed you the wedding pictures . . ." Even if I remember, I always act like the one who doesn't remember anything. "With age, you know, my good friend, if I'm not careful, I'll end up forgetting my own name." Since frequently I don't have any choice, I accept the kiss of Judas, knowing full well that the fawning hypocrite will never return. At times, though, I have had to invent a case of the flu, coughing as if my thorax was about to detach, so that I didn't have to feel her lips, enhanced with a set of false teeth bought for the occasion, on my cheeks: "It's better not to arrive with a bad virus in the land of the whites, neighbor. Those heartless people are capable of putting you back on the airplane, only for that, and sending you home . . ." I drive the point home intentionally and eye the shameless woman scornfully as soon

as her back is turned. There is, after all, a time when you have
to know how to send someone packing and not be taken for a
flight attendant, no?

Some of the young people swear that they'll write me at Christ-
mas or at New Year's. A few of them will keep their promise;
the others will perhaps have passed under the Tree of Oblivion.
Generally, around Easter, while I am cooling off on the veranda
with my eyes half-closed, the mailman wakes me up with a toot
of his horn from atop his moped, and, shortly thereafter, my
servant leaves in my hands an envelope or a postcard that my
tired eyes will decipher several hours later.

Sometimes I remember the exact traits of my correspondent,
the circumstances of their departure. Sometimes I try, in vain, to
bring back the name itself from the mist of my memory. Then,
I bore, I rummage, day and night, until I remember it. During
the day, I keep staring at the horizon. Then people, especially
Jonas, think I'm not all there, and yet I'm there as real as the
earth's rotation. I want to say that I am not as far away as that,
except in time, which rebels against my brain. At night, my eyes
merge with the shadows that engulf the room. I recite a rosary,
one by one, for those sons, those godchildren, those sisters,
those friends that I will never see again, while the ocean comes
making waves in my head, diverting me toward times that are
not those of this city, of this earth. Even if I hold it back, put
up dams, it always ends up getting the better of them. Like the
sand castles of our childhood. Sometimes, for weeks at a time,
it lets me pile up stone upon stone, weave my memory, deftly
recover the unfastened snares, before spitefully pouncing on
my stubbornness. Then I imagine the neighborhood, the city,
anemic, emptied of its youth, of its blood. Who will sing the
wake of the dead when they are all gone? Who, besides my little
Jonas, will strew flowers on my final resting place?

I will never know why people get up one morning, choose to
close the door and to wander far from their native land. Leaving behind them relatives, friends, the smell of a neighborhood
without knowing what difficulties they'll run into over there.
I'll never really understand. I mean, without all those pretexts

THE OTHER SIDE OF THE SEA

that you invent or that others, that life, provide. I'm harsh, aren't I? It's my deepest-held feeling, though. In my opinion, you always have the choice, even the one of leaving definitively, of leaving behind this valley of tears. Without a doubt, the real reason for all that is the fear of the Grand Departure. The desire to take advantage of one's stay on earth before the last sound of the bell inviting us to leave for the other shore . . . In the beginning, there was God moving above the waters. In the beginning, there was the ocean . . .

THE CITY

Perched up on a bucket turned upside down near a pile of garbage and wearing a multicolored tie, the man is dripping with sweat. Beige because of the dirt, his shirt collar probably hasn't met with water since the Flood. The veins of his neck taut, ready to explode, he is shouting angrily into a megaphone. Spurts of spit, as big as horseflies, are flying from his mouth. A madman passes near him, makes, with his two hands, an imaginary umbrella he protects his face with, and he laughs, showing saffron-yellow teeth where thick layers of tartar have accumulated. The speaker doesn't pay attention to him and continues preaching in the desert of people and cars that pass by without stopping. From time to time, a man with nothing better to do listens to him half-heartedly. Then the preacher intensifies his efforts and raises his voice. Repent, for the Kingdom of God is at hand! A gullible man approaches the bucket. The man places his hand on the latter's head and baptizes him in the name of the Father, the Son . . . The Holy Ghost is lost in the flow of his words. While carrying out the sacred act, he doesn't forget to solicit other souls for the cause. Remember what happened at Sodom and Gomorrah, where people were wallowing in their sins. There is still time. Soon, the Gates of Grace will be closed.

Jonas watches the man for a while, shakes his head without anyone really knowing what that gesture might mean, before continuing on his way. They were the same apocalyptic words that, every day at dawn, brutally wake him up. Wake up, you who are sleeping! The disciples of Christ fell asleep on the Mount of Olives when they were supposed to be praying. The voice even penetrates into his sleep. Jonas can never fall back to sleep. The neighborhood is used to those booming calls for repentance. Sometimes it's an evening prayer vigil when the good-for-nothings and the hungry come from far away to drone on all night long with loud chants. Sometimes, it's a morning group directed by an ex-torturer who is still living in the mansion built during the period of his glory, and where every room is rented to individuals at a high price. An ever-increasing number of converts come to hear him promise the fire of hell to criminals. Those who possess illegally acquired goods. The rich who don't share with the poor. At the Last Judgment, God will demand an explanation from them. Jonas's grandmother always takes advantage of the situation by getting up, her Bible in hand, and singing some verses with the undesirable neighbors.

Jonas hadn't set foot in that part of the city for ages. None of his friends or relatives lived there. The cultural centers he used to go to had moved. Following the tracks of that student who had been absent from his classes for two weeks, he wound up there again. Having asked at least a half dozen people, he was able to find the house he was looking for. A single room, where a woman, embarrassed, receives him. The student's mother hasn't seen him for several days. She doesn't know; he's not the only one of her children who has left without coming back. She put everything in God's hands. Jonas left the interview disappointed. What was he hoping for from that brief conversation with a woman whose face was evidence of her tough life? As he leaves, he casts a last glance back at the house. It's already a miracle that his student has been able to hold out this long, he says to himself.

The area offers the same state of desolation as the little house. No roads anywhere. Not even space enough to turn around. Makeshift shops spread out on a bit of wood about the size of the palms of your hands. Two or three articles. No more. Small bottles of milk or carbonated beverages, canned food whose labels, between the dirt and the rust, can't be deciphered anymore. One or two small packs of cigarettes, sold individually, that constitute the main part of the vendor's inventory. Bits of hardened bread. Has anyone ever haggled over them with him? Over there, shriveled-up candy, gooey leather due to the sun. Seated behind her display, a woman under the protection of a wide straw hat stretches out her hand, struggles with the wrapping to extract the piece of candy, brings it to her mouth, and sucks vigorously. The young man lowers his head. He doesn't dare look into people's eyes. As if he were responsible for their distress.

Right next to her, young street urchins swoop down on the windows of cars stopped in the traffic jams with waxy rags that make them dirtier. Some drivers chase them away. Others accept a service executed in the twinkling of an eye. They extend a supplicating hand while looking away, embarrassed. The driver drops the coin into a palm, avoiding contact with the filthy hand. Others hit the road looking to survive. A job as a porter. Getting a car out of the mud. Sex, earlier and earlier. Renting your ass to a local or a tourist while closing your eyes hard and clenching your teeth. As long as it allows you to eat afterward, and to buy yourself a patch of land in paradise. Artificial.

With difficulty, Jonas makes his way in the midst of all those people. He's sweating like the others. The sun is burning his head. The desire to vomit constricts his chest. The city is bustling under the sun's fire. Quivering, sex in heat. The city rises and falls. Sweats, labors. Stays congested from morning until night. The city, if you can call it that, this morass where millions of humans live together, and three times as many pigs. All wallowing in the shit. One on top of the other. And that desire to vomit, in the name of God, that never comes to pass. He reels. His gait wavers.

Farther away, the young man sees the cardboard huts clinging to the side of the mountains. In the slightest nooks and crannies. They have cropped up with a disconcerting rapidity, like weeds. In one night. An afternoon. Certain families take turns sleeping there. Amid the rats and the rubbish. And the pigs, too, who've invaded the city. Black ones. Crossbreeds. Multicolored ones. Their snouts lost under the mounds of debris. They scatter them into trails of stench along the roads they cross like divas, followed by a whole multitude of swine swaying their nonchalant fat as if the entire world were watching them pass. In some cultures, it's the cow, a sacred animal, that stops traffic. In others, the eagle deploys its talons as a symbol of power. Elsewhere, the condor passes by in majestic flight. Here, it's the pigs that strut around. As an omen of the shit the city was destined to become. They are everywhere. A perfect imitation of the space that welcomed them. Teeming with mud and pestilence. On the main road. On the side roads. The dirt roads. The shortcuts. The fronts of houses. The first ones to greet

guests at the exit of the airport and welcome them to Shitsville.
You see them inside the central cemetery gorging themselves on
the corpses that the rain and the tomb robbers have snatched
from the shadows of death. No one knows who they belong
to. Except perhaps their owners . . . Lost in his thoughts, Jonas
bumps into a small group of people gathered right in the middle
of the street.

II There are twenty or thirty of them, but it seems as if there
were thousands. They form a circle of hate around the
body curled up on the ground, on the asphalt buckling
under the midday heat. The sun is at its zenith. Their shadows,
merged under their feet in a shifting, deformed ball, resemble
the evil spirits that have taken possession of their heads. Their
expressions reveal something that no longer belongs to the human race. Their eyes send out strange sparks. They scream.
Gesticulate. Each one is brandishing a different weapon: a piece
of wood, an old knife, a chipped bottleneck, unearthed who
knows where and still covered with mud. An enormous stone
generating spasmodic discharges in the frail arms that hold it
above a head with prominent veins. In a few seconds, it'll smash
against the head. It's biding its time.

The body is curled up in a fetal position. The arms are
crossed over the chest, the hands gripping the shoulders as if
seeking protection from the cold. The knees are almost touching the chin. He doesn't have any expression in his eyes anymore. Doesn't he see the crowd demanding his sacrifice? Is he
still thinking? Perhaps he's reviewing his life, not that different
than that of his executioners. Then he says to himself that death
is the best gift they could offer him. Perhaps he's already on the
other side. Floating in the other world. Celebrating his reunion
with the spirit of his childhood. The shades of his ancestors.
He's no longer there, in any case. Not in the middle of their
screaming, of their madness that is demanding a scapegoat to
exorcize their misery and their hunger, to saw off their giant

rats' teeth that gnaw away at hope, to ward off the anguish of living. Hoping that, at the end of the sacrifice, a new sun will rise.

Powerless, Jonas witnesses the ceremony. He'd like to intervene. But what would he say? He'd only be offering them a new lamb. He knows that. Shaken by imperceptible convulsive movements, the body is only allowed to stiffen for brief intervals. In tatters, his T-shirt reveals a chest spattered with blood. A swollen eyeball is hanging out of its socket. The result of the blows received while his executioners were dragging him along the ground, his lips form a puffy whole with the rest of his face. Slaps like there's no tomorrow. A woman threw the contents of a chamber pot in his face. Laughing, a child let fly with a kick to his nose. His nostrils pissed blood. Others pummeled his ribs with billy clubs. As a result, they became numb. In the end, people were beating him, and he didn't feel anything anymore. Who is he? No one could say. A werewolf that gorges itself on the blood of newborn babies. No, he's one of those bourgeois that squeezes people like a lemon. An adulterous woman. Shaken by twitches arriving at regular intervals, the body attempts to lift its head. A boot pins its neck to the ground. The sound of the skull hitting the asphalt is heard. The face is completely disfigured.

"Crush him!"

"Ram the broomstick up his asshole until it comes out of his mouth."

"Bust open his guts to see what he's eaten. Me, I don't have anything to give to my son for lunch."

"Give him what he deserves!"

"Put the 'necklace' on him!"

"I've got some gas."

"Here are some matches."

"Roast him like a badly skinned pig!"

The voices burst forth from all over. And above all those smiles on their faces, the sun is beating down. Perhaps it has mounted the heads of the crowd where it's dancing a diabolical fandango. People pass by on the street without stopping. Cars slow down so as not to hit someone and risk being subjected to the same end. A woman, rather young, elbows her way through the crowd and arrives at the front near the victim. She places her legs above his head. She remains standing and spreads her legs. She lifts her dress. With her index finger, she slides her underpants to one side and urinates in the mouth of the body. The yellowish liquid squirts, foams, and becomes a whitish halo around his face. With the same index finger, she readjusts her underpants, lets her dress fall down over her chronically mal-nourished buttocks, and leaves. She doesn't take two steps be-fore she backtracks and finishes her work with a thick stream of spit propelled by lips twisted with disdain. The crowd rejoices. Two men take her by the waist and toss her into the air. They catch her. The heroine laughs. The ceremony just doesn't end. It seems to follow a ritual unknown to Jonas. Everyone adds a note of improvisation. A macabre jam session under the tropi-cal sun. All that is transformed into a cerebral music capable of waking up thousands of the dead. It's the Last Judgment. Orchestrated by an invisible shaman, the ritual accelerates. Un-screwed from its trunk, the head is delicately lifted, then held up by several hands at the same time. They slip the used tire, which was covering his chest and joined arms, around his neck. For a long minute, the body hasn't breathed. Like time, the crowd is suspended by the sacrificial act. Jonas smells the odor of gaso-line invading the air. He doesn't hear the striking of the match. Only the odor of something singeing. Of charred human flesh.

"Give me a bit to see what it tastes like."

"Look how his stomach is swelling."

"Demons are coming out."

"Don't touch it! It'll put a jinx on you for the rest of your life."

"Let him roast."

"Smell the odor he's giving off."

"I'd say laurel."

"No, it's vetiver."

"Actually, it's My Dream perfume."

It's as if Jonas were paralyzed. His blood refuses to circulate in his veins. What to do? Where to go? His head is going to explode. A throbbing pain. Will he survive what he has seen?

THE CITY

The sparks crackle and merge into the rays of the sun. The crowd is circling around the flame in a dance rhythm. Their feet tear up the softened asphalt. Their faces are suffused with hysterical laughter. Their steps executed as if in slow motion. The body becomes black. Lumps forming in the area of his abdomen explode. The weak sounds of a damp firecracker that only the young man hears. And the odor. He feels it sticking to his skin. Two spindly arms, trembling, drop an enormous stone on the head, which is flattened like a pupil's notebook. A man rushes onto the pyre and plunges his hand into the middle of the flames. He brings out a forearm that is still smoking. He puts it between his teeth before offering a grimacing smile to the lenses of the foreign reporters.

Jonas feels nausea contracting his chest. He cries out: Noooo! No one hears him. The noises of the city drown out his voice. Noises like thousands of hammer blows banging relentlessly. He rushes like a crazy man trying to find a place where he can breathe, where he can emerge from the nightmare. The odor of the charred cadaver follows him. He weaves between cars in a traffic jam that are moving at a snail's pace. He runs, the odor on his tracks. It's not in a hurry; it doesn't have anything else to do. In the meantime, the fire has died out. Jonas is still running, in no particular direction. Bumping into backs and chests, he cuts through the crowd like an Exocet missile. He brakes abruptly, starts up again, and just barely avoids landing in a hole full of swamp water.

Behind him, life has resumed its normal course. On the concrete, there is a shriveled-up object, burned to a cinder, that has a vaguely human form. The cars drive around it, slowing down traffic even more. Angry, impatient honks. Some drivers get out of their cars. A policeman shows up, followed by a street sweeper, found while he was taking a nap under a tree. The former orders him to take the object away in his wheelbarrow. The man executes the orders using a chipped shovel and an old broom. The object makes a metallic noise when it falls into the wheelbarrow. Traffic becomes fluid again. A few meters away, there is a pile of garbage at the corner of a street. Some piglets are bivouacked there in complete tranquility. They withdraw as the street sweeper approaches. He dumps the object on the garbage pile and dusts off his wheelbarrow with his broom before starting off again. The piglets return and pounce on it. Amid other rubbish, the object crackles in their jaws.

Looking for someplace quiet, Jonas keeps running so as not to hear, hammering in his head, the hysterical shouts of the crowd. The same crowd he identified with for years during ardent discussions with his friends from high school, and later from university. The same one that incarnates the essence of community. Take away the people and there would be nothing left of this city. From the middle class and the bourgeoisie, we others are pale reflections of Western civilizations. Voices bereft of all human expression strike his eardrums. The squealing of those men and women he wonders if he has ever had anything in common with. The crackling of the charred body. Ridding yourself of the odor. His eyes sweep over the stream of cars. Their exhaust fumes catch in his throat. A private place. He realizes that there aren't any in this city. An army of beggars living one on top of the other. Teeming with sweat and grumbling. Rats, that's what they are. Cursed, stinking rats.

The pedestrians merge with the automobiles, which crash into the wheelbarrow drivers, who barely avoid bowling over the stalls of the food vendors, who are stirring, at ground level in the mud swarming with worms and microbes, food above which dogs fart while stepping jauntily over it. Grimy individuals come and wolf it down while turning their backs to the street so as not to be seen or to protect their meal from the dust and the stench that have taken possession of the city. Thus, it wasn't the odor of the charred corpse. It's the city that stinks. That smells bad. That's dirty. Ugly. The voice of the dead singer comes back to him. It's true that there's nothing to love there. Nothing to be proud of. The voice of the singer who denigrates loving too much. And who doesn't love anymore. And then that odor. The ever-present desire to vomit.

THE CITY

||| Jonas spent the whole afternoon running. It's very late now. It gets late fairly early these days. In a few minutes, there won't be a soul on the streets. People are hurrying as if a curfew or a flood had been announced. From the beginning of his migraines, caused by the odor and the noises of the city, Jonas only finds respite at night. That's when he feels good. As if the day and its processions of beggars, the indifferent, rubbish, dirt, arrogant luxury, and nauseating scenes repulsed him. A sudden disgust at the daily occurrences, the people he rubs shoulders with, and especially that feeling of no longer swimming in his natural element under the rays of the sun. The night, he knows, belongs to the gangsters, to the cops who are at their beck and call. But the prostitutes animate it, too, the poets, life's castaways, a whole slice of humanity with dreams as long as the Amazon River. Thus, in spite of the growing dangers, he likes crisscrossing it, letting himself go in a pleasant drift that often leads to his encountering its marginal people and the sadness lurking in the depth of their eyes.

Jonas continues his stroll in a night riddled with the intermittent sounds of hammers, but he decides to ignore them and take full advantage of his reprieve. The more he walks, the more his mind clears. A gust of oxygen, having originated from the soles of his feet, rises up to his brain. He feels light. There's a nip in the air. A dog, all skin and bones, is moving its snout along the gutter looking for supper. A pig's grunt a few meters away gets him to turn his head. A black car that looks like a hearse passes him by, a concert of loose nuts and bolts piercing the night's massive veil. The sky is strewn with hundreds of stars. Jonas has fun counting them, then he abandons the idea . . . The young man would be incapable of saying how he arrived there. Everything is floating in his head, misty like undesirable memories. In fact, he rejects the only points of reference he has at his disposal. The rapid degradation of the things around him. The absence of combativeness in the faces: people staggering, dazed. Knocked out but standing. And the incapacity, from then on, to reconcile his own ambitions with collective dreams.

Near the police station, Jonas recognizes the Passport Man, as he and his friends called him in their early adolescence. He always carried an expired passport, three-quarters torn, clearly visible in the pocket of his jacket dirty enough to scare a garbage collector. In one hand, he is holding an old suitcase, full of holes and stuffed with various assorted objects. He stops Jonas and asks him the time. I can't miss my plane. You know, people are always late in this city, and the planes, they aren't trucks leaving for a neighboring town: they don't wait. He continues chattering for a while, then he shakes Jonas's hand. I really have to leave you this time. Be strong, my friend. Don't cry. I will write you. The man raises his finger, hails an imaginary taxi, and moves on with an awkward gait, bent over, encumbered by the weight of his suitcase and the stories circulated about him.

He might have been a Don Juan, spending his time exploiting the gullibility of girls, until one day he fell madly in love with a mulatto with an abundant mane of hair. But she allegedly had to leave him and go abroad because of pressure from her parents, who didn't want him for her: he was too black, and, even worse, he didn't have any money. Since then, he only lived to rejoin her over there. Never having had the means nor the opportunity to obtain a visa, he allegedly lost all contact with reality. It was enough to cite the girl's name and tell him that she had married a white man with eyes the color of the ocean to drive him stark-raving mad. Or to moping in a corner shedding copious tears. Others say he was linked to political activities and that, the vice tightening around him, he was getting ready to take refuge in a neighboring country when he was arrested at the airport, imprisoned, and tortured. When he was released from prison, his sanity was gone. Are we to believe those for whom he was the eldest son of a family of nine children? After having sold their meager possessions, his parents gave him the money to buy a visa. All the hopes of the family were resting on his departure; he was supposed to bring the others on board. But he liked games of chance too much. Thinking he could multiply his assets, he entered a casino and came back out at five in the morning with only the clothes on his back. And even that, according to the rumors, is because they weren't brand names. He couldn't accept having blown his family's chance and seeing them stagnate in the misery of a shantytown because of his unhealthy passion. Jonas watches the man disappear into the night before continuing his solitary walk in the city where the hammer blows seem to have intensified their fervor. Bang! Bang! Bang!

IV Jonas is walking in the city penetrated by a distant song, a melody full of fatalism and determination at the same time. "Si n pa mouri nan dlo, si nou pa neye o/Bondye bon n a rive lòtbòdlo . . ." Where did it get it? From the night dotted with the flickering glow of a few hurricane lamps? From the sky studded with stars? Without a doubt the hammer blows were endowed with a vital energy the likes of which the young man had never experienced before. Bang! Bang! Bang! The blows are becoming louder and louder. And closer. It's as if the entire city were singing in his head. "Lè nou rive, yo mande n sa n pote o/N pa pot anyien, men nou kapab travay o . . ." Jonas looks around him, but except for the repeated blows of the hammer, no one, no sound is disturbing the atmosphere. He is walking alone in the city in spite of the tacit curfew imposed by the gangs and the occult forces that share power. Those who mix mysticism with a thirst for material goods, who combine brute force with muddled ideological discourse.

The night is white. The entire city is given over to fear. To the rare police patrols, Jonas responds that he's going home, that he wasn't able to find public transportation. One of the patrols, in a show of politeness, offers to take him there. The idea of finding himself in the back end of a pickup truck surrounded by cops armed as if they were leaving for war startles the young man. He responds no, thank you. I'm almost there. It's at the intersection over there. And he points his finger toward the dark horizon. The vehicle has barely turned the corner when shots ring out in the distance. Crisp shots, followed by

THE OTHER SIDE OF THE SEA

longer detonations, then silence. Two or three minutes later, they pick up again. Probably gangs preparing to operate with total impunity shooting to announce their arrival; in that way, people won't put up any resistance. Sometimes, emotion dictates unpredictable reactions, and the young gangsters don't like to kill without a reason. Moreover, the policemen can move into a different zone; they aren't paid for all those minutiae. But sometimes, some of them accept a confrontation, as was the case last week. An outburst of professional consciousness, of patriotism: we have to rid the city of that scourge.

The shots have stopped. Jonas hears the clicking of his heels on the sidewalk, like a nocturnal companion. That takes him back fifteen years when, as a child, he would have to go out at night to run an errand for his grandmother. He would sing at the top of his lungs so that everyone in his entourage stayed wide awake. Thus, he wasn't alone. The zombies, the werewolves, and other beasts without names knew it and made way for him. At night, a dog is never a dog, and the cats are black. Their eyes sparkle in a way not usually seen during the day. They can continue watching you for a long time, sometimes follow you during your entire trip. Even if you turn back and throw a stone at them, they just turn their heads away and continue to follow you.

Approaching a belt of misery, the young man comes upon a semblance of life. From around a hurricane lamp, which is emitting a pallid flame, and a fried-fish stand virtually empty, voices are dispersed into the night. They all are speaking at once, and with the same gusto, until one of them gets the better of the others by telling a joke. A light breeze takes the bursts of laughter and scatters them into the air. Where do they get the courage to laugh? People with nothing to lose, no doubt. They have never had anything and thumb their noses at fear, at crime. Jonas greets the small group—some men, a few women, two or three children half asleep between the legs of the adults—and continues on his way. He wanders a long while without encountering any other human presence, rerunning, in his head, the film of the city's last ten years. The night is white, and black. The rare streetlights working project a pale light that is lost somewhere in space before reaching the ground. Light has been dependent, for a very long time, on the caprices of the hydraulic dam, on the goodwill of the rain. (Too much rain falls, or not enough. When there is too much, it fills the reservoirs with mud.) Dependent on the gasoline, always too expensive, to make the generators work. On the missing parts that have to be imported from abroad. On the national electric company. On its director. On its striking employees.

The shots have started up again, alternating with the bang! bang! of the hammers. Ta ta ta / bang bang. Ta ta ta. Perhaps it's police officers, disguised in civilian clothes, supplementing their end-of-the-month paycheck by helping themselves to a neighborhood. No one enters and no one leaves. Trucks are filled that will leave for an unknown destination. Perhaps it's gangs confronting each other for the control of an area or the control of a market in arms or knives. The next day the news will be diffused throughout the city. The grapevine. The media. The offices. Certain people will testify in place of the victims, stabbed with seventeen knife wounds. Others, riddled with bullets, unrecognizable sieves lying in their own blood. Girls raped. One of them is a virgin. The rapist thanks her for that gift from heaven and violates her innocence with a brutal pelvic thrust. A three-month-old girl brandished at arm's length like a sacrificial lamb. The thief, looking for cocaine, quarters her in front of her mother's eyes. The little girl's blood splashes the face of the man, who wipes it off with the back of a hand.

The resonance of Jonas's heels on the sidewalk, mixed with the hammer blows and the shots of automatic weapons, compose a strange symphony in three movements. His heels click, the hammers bang, the bullets crackle. And the questions bang around inside his head. The blasts ending up getting the upper hand. Perhaps the occult forces that add a layer of terror to the population's despair. Later, they will present themselves as saviors. Waiting, the city holds its breath. In a few hours, there will be light, but there still won't be anyone on the streets. A strike has been called. Labor unions and working-class organizations know how to dissuade those with cold feet and those preventing rotating strikes. We should export the recipe, Jonas thinks: pulverized windshields, cars set on fire, occupants dying of fear before being beat up. Jonas will walk in the city, white with fear. The stores' shutters will be lowered. The street vendors won't need to fool misery and will have to find other arms to kill time with. Police patrols, a few press cars, as well as those of international organizations, will crisscross the streets like that night. Continuing to sway with their indolent gait, the pigs won't be aware of anything except the reduced noise and tire screeching when they eat. The strike will be a success. Jonas wonders for whom.

It's four o'clock in the morning. Exhausted, Jonas returns home to sleep. Sleep doesn't come. The questions are still floating, phantoms of darkness upon the entrance of light. He can't sleep anymore. He doesn't want to sleep anymore. It's the same thing since he encounters the same questions. I'm afraid of sleep like one is afraid of a big hole, full of a vague horror, leading who knows where. His migraine and his fever have already taken possession of his being. The armada is advancing, sweeping his lucidity away with one flick. This time, that's it: his reason is taking off. His brain is out of order like the antiquated mechanism of a clock. Sleep . . . The hammer blows. Bang! Bang! Bang! Thousands of hammers that are banging, banging, banging, without knowing if they are pinning down crime or constructing hope. Sleep, animated by a thousand and one nightmares.

V Jonas's sleep is less uneven now. The nightmares are giving way to the face of his grandmother. "I swear that (pardon me, dear God), while I'm alive, no one in my family will leave the shores of this city. We were born here, and we have our roots here. Even dead, we will refuse to leave it." Age has bowled the old woman's head over to the other side of reason. For ages she's continued to repeat the same refrain drawn from a life full of sound and fury. It's her only immutable link with reality, into which she enters and from which she leaves according to her moments of lucidity, the rambling of an insomniac, long soliloquies that keep her alive at more than eighty, ninety years old. The young man doesn't know her exact age. He isn't interested in knowing it, either, other than that she's been there forever and will be there forever. She's eternal.

Jonas likes to touch her fissured face, furrowed, crossed with so many wrinkles that have traced all sorts of arabesques on it. Curiously, her skin is not sagging. It's not exactly firm, but it's not turning into limp flesh, either. It's as if she had decided once and for all to resist the ravages of age. She is always very clean and smells like talcum powder after her bath, which she takes behind the house, seated on an old chair with the straw missing, which lets her withered buttocks through, while her servant, equipped with a chipped beaker, pours water over her head. Now and then, Jonas takes the soap, slips onto her back, and his hands, those of a man then, search, on the emaciated breasts of the old woman that have merged with her thorax, for the smells of his childhood, when his head would sink down between two very soft cushions. And she, who was rather gruff in her affection, pretends to scold him, asks him what he's looking for in those empty old wineskins. Don't you see there's nothing left . . .

Grannie, as Jonas calls her, never strays more than a meter from the veranda (in any case, she isn't able to go any farther), where passers-by bring her the news from elsewhere, from everywhere, from nowhere. She comments on it with assurance, as if in her head she were keeping, like in a shabby old notebook, a registry of the names of all those who had left, of their destinations, that, to be honest, she is unaware of. But she has always known how to allay suspicion, let her interlocutor talk in order to gather the information necessary to continue the conversation: at that game, she would fool even the devil on the date of his fall from paradise . . .

And then, there's her faltering memory to remind her, in flashes of reason, of the time when the clamor of trains filled the city, the city of days gone by. Everywhere, the houses are repainted at New Year's. The beautiful main artery is empty of people and of cars. The city, conscious of its appearance like a fiancée at her approaching wedding. And many other things in her absent stare that no one, besides Jonas, would know how to pick up on. How many times has she evoked them in the presence of the young man, as a warning, or talking to herself, to ward off the fantasies of elsewhere that, who knows, perhaps aren't completely extinguished inside of her? It was enough for him to raise his eyes toward her face to hear them banging inside her head like those inside an unhealthy drum. With that bittersweet cadence of the forbidden, of guilt.

Today, Grannie is practically crippled from the time that she fell into a manhole left uncovered right in the middle of the sidewalk. One afternoon of rain had been enough to transform the city into a torrent. The water had ripped off the drainage cover, and someone had carried it away to do who knows what. The gaping hole, exhaling the pestilence of the accumulated refuse, had remained there for several months. Jonas's grandmother hadn't seen it and landed amid the fruit peelings, provisions in a state of advanced decomposition, remnants of food, dead rats, fecal matter. Pulled by three men, she was extricated from it, albeit with contusions, a dislocated leg, and above all, that smell, which took her more than a week to get rid of; it was like the one Jonas had brought back from the lower part of the city. It took several daily baths with green leaves, a cake of household soap, and the patience of the servant to get rid of it.

Jonas's grandmother refuses to admit it, but she's getting older. She doesn't have the same means at her disposal as before when she would work like a maniac so that her grandson was never lacking anything, when she would rise up, like a giant barricade, against all adversity that could threaten him. She would frequently stop work at two o'clock in the morning and pick up again at dawn with the first imprecations of the preachers, the singing of the street vendors, with the sun's rays filtering through the blinds. But that period is over, and above all her sight isn't much use to her anymore. Just barely good enough to examine what she eats before she puts it in her mouth. The manhole is, though, as visible as the baldness of the mountains that encircle the city and let water inundate it with every storm. She, however, didn't see it. Or perhaps at the last minute, when it was too late. That handicap had already brought about her being hit by a car. She couldn't have not seen it. That's what the driver was thinking, too, and he didn't step on the brake in time.

Jonas was going to work when he saw the crowd. It's a common thing here where people, with nothing to do for the most part, are on the lookout for entertainment, to kill time, to fool the hunger humming in their guts. Having approached out of pure curiosity, Jonas saw his grandmother lying unconscious on the ground. She recovered from it with her leg in a cast, the same one that she'd dislocated in her fall into the sewer. The lenses of her glasses were smashed to bits. They have since been replaced, but that doesn't prevent her from bending, more and more, over her daily chapter of the Bible. When she does, she curses the small type. Interrupted every five minutes about the precise meaning of such and such a word, Jonas finds himself reading an entire passage each time, and he ended up becoming her appointed reader. In his absence, the old woman calls on a boy from the neighborhood and corrects him at the first mispronounced word . . .

That woman, whom Jonas had always known to be as tough as a rock, with energy to spare, thinking up work for herself so as not to remain idle, the person toward whom he instinctively turns in difficult moments, even if they don't talk to each other. That *poteau-mitan* of his life. Now she's collapsing before his very eyes. In her inactivity she seems even older. For many years, she had allayed suspicion; then, time caught up with her. All at once. Capital and interest included. It was Jonas's turn to support her. He is all she has . . . Her image floats a few instants more in front of the young man's eyes before the nightmares regain possession of his sleep.

JONAS'S STORY

I was still busy growing up when the city started resonating with the incessant hammer blows, rising in a crescendo like a harmonic note played a tone higher than the rest of the music, that would determine life's rhythm on this side of the ocean. No doubt it had all begun well before that evening. No doubt the hammering was picking up again after a long pause, like waves receding before launching themselves more spitefully against the hull of a fragile boat. In any case, it was at that moment that I started to hear them. I remember the crisp, timid sound of the first blow very well, then the second. The third was already more determined . . . I jumped out of bed and went over toward the window that I often kept open to let the sleep-facilitating breeze in, and I pricked up my ears. The strange, exasperating drums were amplified during the night and continued on until daylight. They haven't stopped since, drowning out all other noises in the vicinity: the racket of the cars, the screams of lovemaking, the cries of hungry children, the furor of the sun, the muffled steps of memory . . .

Then, the city belonged to the son of the man-who-had-taken-power-for-a-thousand-years. The population had ended up getting used to the idea and would watch him, with a certain indulgence, drag his easygoing figure around the palace courtyard, to the point of forgetting the years of terror that had characterized his father's reign. Of course, the day after some particularly irreverent carnival-like festivities relating to his own reign, he appeared on television bellowing that he was the son of a tiger and that, on occasion, he knew how to demonstrate his natural reflexes, but no one took him seriously. The population had only taken advantage of his appearance on television to name him Titig, a rather affectionate diminutive like those one encounters so often in this corner of the world. Subsequently, the city's inhabitants even greeted his marriage with a former stripper as well as the birth of the last member of the dynasty with jubilation. Only a high-caliber seer would have been able to predict what was going to follow.

In point of fact, the sudden disappearance of Marie-Claire, who had initiated all the pimply adolescents in the neighborhood in the pleasures of the flesh, should have awakened the suspicions of at least the youngest of those she was terrorizing solely by the power of her sex. But we were living too much in the memory of her lessons to think about anything else. Not even about the casual, and rather frustrating, pedagogy of this woman five years our elder. We had to pretend to understand when, according to selection criteria known only by her mood at the moment, she had set her heart on one of us for a morning or an afternoon. Proud and drooling with impatience, the one chosen would follow her then. Sometimes, the same day, she would take someone else, who would leave strutting about, too, but ready to return with his tail between his legs if ever she'd look at him askance.

We would often get together to evoke her charms, to spar verbally about who had given her the most pleasure. We all knew she kept the truth in her impassive countenance that watched from the window for the inopportune arrival of an intruder, while our adolescence worked itself to death behind her dress, raised just above the buttocks, in pursuit of that spasm shaking our bodies from head to toe that we used to reach through masturbation and that, with her, would always arrive in less time than was needed to unfasten the pants she never allowed us to take completely off. Afterward, we had to hurry up and get dressed while she remained planted in front of us, like an easygoing watchman, her face suffused with a strange grin, her elbow leaning on the windowsill. Her flawless vigilance didn't, though, prevent her sister from surprising us one morning making love. I can't believe it! What is this, this impertinence? she exclaimed. I barely had time to pull up my pants and rush out of the room, followed by the voice of the young woman bawling out her younger sister.

After that misadventure, which made me the laughingstock of all my friends, Marie-Claire distanced herself from us. She would hardly ever go out. We only saw her leaving to run her errands before shutting herself up in the room she was sharing with her older sister. By looking intently through the same shutters she used to watch for intruders, I caught sight of her one day stretched out on her bed as naked as she was the day she was born. Her nudity, which I was discovering for the first time, intrigued me less than the absent, distorted expression of her face, though. Perhaps someone had informed her of a catastrophe: the death of her parents, the end of the world in twenty-four hours without her having been able to understand its essence. Like that adolescent girl who, after a pastor's convincing sermon on the imminent return of Christ, went secretly to pray to Christ to ask him to delay his coming long enough so that she, too, could savor the mysteries of marriage. Marie-Claire was humming an old song that, in the city, the families passed on from generation to generation and that, in the last analysis, no one knew the origin nor the author of. The song came solemnly from her lips while sad tears were rolling over her round face.

> Blow, wind! Blow, wind!
> My mother has sailed
> My father has sailed
> Blow, blow!
> I will see them.

Marie-Claire disappeared one morning without leaving a trace. Some said that she had forded the Massacre River, returning to the town next to it, the one she came from. For others, she had taken one of those small boats that were attempting to reach the shores over there, a stowaway on a fateful journey where, from the start, she was seated on the bench. Still others circulated the rumor of her death during a ceremony in which she was getting ready to sell her soul to Lucifer in exchange for a position as a madam and the renown that would accompany it. At the appearance of the devil, she didn't, in spite of the master of ceremonies' warning, resist her desire to look him in the face. She opened her eyes and died, thunderstruck, even before having been able to close them. As for me, one single question continues to haunt my mind: why would she give herself to inexperienced teenagers of fourteen, fifteen years old like us when she had the necessary charm to seduce men much more mature? For a long time, I hoped to bump into her somewhere, by chance, in the streets in a city of millions of anonymous inhabitants. I would have invited her to make love in a hotel room, on the beach, behind the bushes. I would have loved her for her generosity and for the adolescents of the neighborhood, for all those to whom she had offered both hell and paradise in the sinkhole between her thighs. I still haven't abandoned that hope.

||||||||||||||||||||||||||||||||||||||||||||||||||||||||||||||||||||||||||||||||||||||||||||||||||||||||||||||||||||

the wind oh the wind in the sails drenched with blood the wind tossing those eyes from top to bottom riveted on the surface of darkness and broken dreams not knowing the depth of the sea the only unique possessor of the absolute in the world oh the wind filled with the silence of the night and travelers forced by which lunar consort one will never know nor by which wind in the bowsprit nor if it was night's arm of course dawn tucked away in its lights but reclaiming with one hand what it erased with the other

oh the wind from the interior of lands that didn't know the water's protean nature nor its existence nor that the earth pushed by its valor was turning oh the wind meeting the waters writing the night like a long flow of misery the wind oh and those arms of dawn-night to carry us toward a new land the wind without the slightest remembrance of their clumsy stories

||||||||||||||||||||||||||||||||||||||||||||||||||||||||||||||||||||||||||||||||||||||||||||||||||||||||||||||||||||

The disappearance of Marie-Claire was the only real point of reference I had at my disposal to situate the hammer blows in time. From that date on, and especially at night when, stretched out on my bed, I was dreaming of her lost charms, it was as if an evil spirit had announced to the population in a dream that the city was going to be razed to the ground. From morning till night, the handsaws were frenetically busy, trees were cut down, planks sawn, and there was banging, there was banging. The city had been transformed into an enormous construction site that wasn't far from resembling our planet in the days preceding the Flood. In one neighborhood, not one single tree remained, the earth was parched and giving way, before one's very eyes, to the advance of the desert. Entire families had constructed lightweight boats that could barely manage to stay above water and left without paying their respects to the gods, nor turning their heads around, for fear of being turned into statues of salt. In another one, its inhabitants were selling everything they possessed, liquidated for only the price of the crossing. Some were even obliged to add loans from their parents, or from their friends, to raise the required amount.

Not one week went by without a small wooden boat, filled to the brim with men and women whose ragged bodies, dried out by the sun and salt, contrasted with their eyes sparkling with hope, being inspected on the high seas. Those who had been successful in escaping the attention of the coast guard's vessels or bribing its agents were not, however, sure of arriving intact. Quite often, the fragile skiffs capsized a few miles farther out, overturned by the first groundswell or the first reef encountered. The sea would open, swallow the passengers, then close up over them before regaining its indolence. No survivors. In the best of cases, the boat would run aground on other shores than the ones promised or dreamed of. On the big island. On the myriads of stones scattered in the middle of the ocean. Sometimes the captain himself would choose, by lot, the men to throw overboard to lighten the boat or to sacrifice in order to appease the wrath of the gods. Women wouldn't have their lives spared unless they knew how to silence certain scruples. Thus, a new breed of entrepreneur was born that rushed into the organization of trips whose passengers, besides having paid a lot for the crossing, were robbed of their few belongings and thrown to the sharks.

Doubting perhaps the efficiency of his repression and worried about his image abroad, the son-of-the-man started paying people so they wouldn't leave. His wife would distribute the envelopes from slum to slum herself, where she was cheered as the new Evita. More than one person proposed sending a mission to the Vatican in order to have her canonized in spite of her past as a stripper. Her hagiographers maintained that she couldn't have done anything worse than Mary Magdalene.

The leaders from over there were quick to imitate the couple. Moreover, their gifts were accompanied by experts who came to teach the population the art of calming their desire to leave. Some quickly squandered in revelry the money gained in that way. For them, the exodus signaled the beginning of the end of the world. Better to enjoy yourself to your heart's content, especially if you weren't sure of entering paradise. For several days, the city's seedier neighborhoods took on the look of a modern-day Sodom. Men and women changed beds, in a debauchery of food, music, perfume, and exotic drinks. Inhabitants of high society came to mix with the riffraff without the slightest concern for their social status. While the others were frolicking in their forbidden games, the shrewd ones were gathering money together from every possible source to finance new boats.

To dissuade the most stubborn people, unbearable, to say the least, scenes were shown on television. A shark finishing off a pregnant woman in a single mouthful. The fetus, which was still attached by its umbilical cord, was snapped up by the same thrust of the jaw. Those who managed to arrive over there were welcomed by soldiers armed from head to foot, brutally manhandled with billyclubs after having scarcely set foot on shore. Those who survived that treatment landed in internment camps where doctors little preoccupied with professional ethics were delighted by the guinea pigs placed at their disposition. Men left the camps transformed into women with two enormous nipples in the middle of their chests. The women saw an ugly beard growing on their chins and their breasts melt like butter in the sun after a treatment of three daily injections of androsterone. Those monsters, formerly human beings, were also shown on television. But nothing worked. Persuaded that the other shore couldn't be worse than their city, people continued to leave. No place could be worse than their city.

From the height of her rocking chair installed on the veranda, Grannie didn't stop grousing upon seeing her neighborhood unravel like a ball of yarn. Her pain was even greater upon learning that people we knew were part of the wreckage. In an endless litany, she would murmur, Why?, as if overcome by the events. Why doesn't anyone tell them that they won't find anything over there, not even the echo of their dreams? Then she would become even sadder than the lid of the tomb she was getting closer to day by day. I had never before noticed all those wrinkles on her face, nor her head covered with a shock of hair, very white, from which several rare strands of grey stood out. The rest seemed to have shot up in one night. She was shriveling up, almost bent in two, having lost that stature, slender and proud, that made me compare her to Peul women from distant Africa. And her mouth, with its sunken cheeks for lack of teeth since she didn't wear her false teeth willingly, repeating, as if addressing only herself, Why?

The same question that she would ask me if ever I'd return an hour later than we'd anticipated. Hardly had she heard the key's noise in the lock of the entrance. Is that you? Who else would you like it to be, Grannie? Aren't you sleeping? How do you think I could sleep with all that is going on? And you, why are you coming back so late? Immutable ritual. Sometimes, I would go and sit down on the edge of her bed and chitchat with her for a while. Following the grooves on her face, I would go back in time. She could spend the whole night rummaging through her memory if I didn't pay attention. Telling me about those times when there was a city. Now all that is very distant, my little Jonas. But you shouldn't be afraid: it's the fulfillment of the prophecy. The reign of men will end; the return of Christ is nigh . . .

|||||||||||||||||||||||||||||||||||||||||||||||||||||||||||||||||||||||||||||||||||||||||||||||||||||||||||||||||||||||||||||||||||

    the lack of air the suffocation the odor of vomit mixed with the flatulence that escapes from intestines with fetid breaths with the foul smell of rotten cod from armpits and crotches from successive layers of dried sweat on the skin the mold of bodies the open mouth seeking breaths of adulterated oxygen the deterioration of certain pieces of wood merges with the decomposition of dozens of rats' cadavers that heads or aggressive hooves have crushed against the walls mildewed with rotten fish from the sea filtering through the interstices smells of males and females mixed the stuffiness hold in bursts of odor spraying

the passengers above invisible smoke that stings the nostrils of
those ladies animal odor

|||||||||||||||||||||||||||||||||||||||||||||||||||||||||||||||||||||||||||||||||||||||||||||||||||||||||||||||||||||||||||

Those leaving took with them, like a relic to guarantee the
crossing, a song composed by a troubadour whose name no
one knew. A song as if born of the entrails of the sea, of the vain
suffering of those who disappeared and of the indelible hope of
the survivors. The latter asserted that they had traveled with the
author, who was alleged to have improvised it scarcely a couple
of minutes before disappearing amid the waves. They had allegedly vowed to him to sing it as long as they had a breath
of life. The city's rulers had good reason to think that it had
germinated in the very heart of the belts of misery where the
composer, protected by an army of beggars and people starv-
ing to death, was hiding and moving from hut to shack. At all
cost, they had to extirpate the song from there, uproot it before
other seeds fell into the earth, so that they didn't grow into as
many trees of life. The mud, the garbage, the fecal matter constituted a first-class fertilizer. So, at night they swept down into
those labyrinths of despair, trampling the dreams of the youngest, tearing couples who were deceiving misery away from one
another, in the midst of the squealing of rats and the cries of
human beings.

During that period, people continued to make one-way trips
and to board small boats with names that were often premoni-
tory (*Straight Toward Death, God Protect Us*). And they would
sing with all the force of their hope. They sang chopping down
the trees, while constructing their canoe, before leaving, on the
raging sea, plunging into the depths of the ocean, upon arrival,
they would sing even when they didn't have their voices anymore, anemic, dehydrated, under the blows from the billyclubs
of the soldiers over there, under the stream of their spit, under
their boots, behind their electrified barbed wire . . . As if the
song contained their entire life, was their life.

> Sou lanmè n ape flote
> N pa menm konnen ki bò n a prale

JONAS'S STORY

Sou lanmè n ape flote
N pa menm konnen ki bò n pral tonbe

Si n pa tonbe nan dlo
Si nou pas neye o
Bondye bon n a rive lòtbòdlo
Si n pa mouri nan dlo
Si nou pas neye o
Bondye bon n a janbe lòtbòdlo

And the boats filled the ocean, defied its fury, defied the laws here and those over there, driven by the dreams of hundreds of thousands of men and women, those who were leaving and those who had stayed, waiting until a brother, a sister, a fiancé, a friend sent for them. They didn't even have enough time to cry for those who'd disappeared. One had to arrive for them, too. The anguish of waiting for days, for a possible telegram, for a cassette with the voice of someone dear to them recounting the odyssey, how, after the shipwreck, he escaped death by latching onto a piece of a wooden plank: the days of drifting, thirst, his throat on fire, hunger, the sun, fainting followed by waking up hours later, the struggle with a small shark that finally ended up withdrawing thanks to his determination, then the deserted beach, the arrival of curious people, of the police, the camp, but the Good Lord, well, one morning, he snuck them away, rescued them from the barbed wire, from the whistles, the gunfire and the billyclubs. The cassette prompted streams of tears in the family, the fear, after the fact, of the danger just barely avoided, the joy in knowing he'd arrived, while their neighbor has been waiting six months for a sign of her son.

Lè nou rive yo mande n sa n pote o
N pa pot anyien men nou kapab travay o
Lè nou rive yo di n pa sa rete o
Y ede oun lòt pouki yo pa ede n tou?

And there was the banging, that banging. In spite of those brought back in ropes, escorted by agents of foreign coast guards who accompanied them right up onto the wharf. Distraught ghosts having left the flame in their eyes, unless it was extinguished forever, along the shore, sighted, but which they, like Moses and the Promised Land, couldn't set foot on. They were carrying a meager bundle of possessions on their backs—their entire fortune in this earthly world—and proceeding with difficulty in a city they didn't seem familiar with anymore. Often, they didn't remember anymore where they were living before their departure. The policemen released them on the street, where they added to the stream of beggars and the homeless, procreated, lived from hand to mouth, disappeared, dragging their aspirations for the other shore into limbo. A long time later, the sea would cast a mauled body on the shore, a skeleton whitened by the salt water, which they had trouble identifying as a brother, a sister, a friend, but it was that of a living Christian like any other, so they buried it, hoping and praying that its soul would return over there. To Guinea.

And Grannie would ask herself, Why? Two rivulets of tears, which she didn't try to retain, would slide into the beautiful wrinkles of her face, filling furrow after furrow, hanging from her chin before falling onto her knees with a muted sound. Why? As for me, I understood too well why, during that entire period, Grannie refused to eat, letting herself waste away before my very eyes. She would play with her dish like a child who isn't hungry, stir the food, mash it, perhaps without even realizing it, to the point of reducing it to porridge. She who had taught me never to throw out the food of our Good Lord. Besides, it's the sweat of men, the fruit of their labor. Don't ever forget that! She, who would always put a plate aside in case someone dropped in, a relative, a friend, someone unknown, it didn't matter. Sometimes I would move closer to her and talk to her about something entirely different before grabbing the spoon and forcing her to swallow two or three mouthfuls. It was better than nothing. Seeing that I had discovered her game, she would open her mouth, smiling. Then, for a while, she accepted a meal a day, continuing all the while, between two streams of tears, to ask out loud, Why? As if those preparing to leave could hear her and renounce their enterprise.

JONAS'S STORY

III Powerlessly, my adolescence was witnessing all those events when Maïté entered my life. It was right in the middle of the month of July. In the company of the other guys, I was killing the long hot days of summer vacation with endless chitchat. To the usual conversations: girls, the very latest kung fu . . . we added our discussions about the departures, the number of which had increased from year to year in the neighborhood: Le Pape, Pouchon, Nanasse, Choupou, Bouboule, and many others, the list of which slipped our minds at times. More than one didn't return, leaving behind an image, a laugh, a joke, a tic, the swerve of a dribble, a shout, that were fading into the ebb and flow of time. Sometimes, a vacationer would report having bumped into one of them. He had put on weight and passed along his greetings to everyone—*everything-somebody,* as Grannie would have said—but he hadn't been able to meet all of them because it's big over there, it's not like here. Each neighborhood is a country all by itself.

The day of Maïté's arrival—truth be told, she had arrived the previous night. That's what explains why we hadn't seen her before, because no new occurrence on the terrain between the sports center and the police station could escape our vigilance. Thus, the following day, my friends and I had taken refuge under a scrawny mahogany tree, trying, with difficulty, to escape the sun's heat. We were evoking, yet again, the golden age of our neighborhood: the soccer teams when Beausoleil, Gary Cordé excelled—and I'm leaving out the best—under the angry whistle of Fritz Madanmango; the best-known romances; the girls (Poupette, Teodora, Delphine, Marie-Michèle) who were its glory and whose fame, having gone beyond our borders, forced us to put into place a strategy to hinder the approach of suitors coming from other neighborhoods. In the space of several hours, the ghosts of those who'd disappeared returned to live among us, laughing, fooling around, as if they hadn't left, teasing one person, who really got worked up, flattering another who was erecting his crest like a rooster in a chicken coop, before regaining the realm known only to them alone. One of us was leaning against the trunk; someone else was sitting on the roots protruding out of the ground, his entire body thrown into the conversation, gestures of his hands, feet, and lower abdomen as well. In the scorching heat of the early afternoon, I suddenly felt something like a breeze: Maïté was passing by, leaving even the most talkative among us speechless.

A trace of light lingered in her wake. Her walk, with its calm cadence and rare elegance, contrasted, I would later learn, with her rather anguished nature. Even when she was late, she never hurried. After having brought her thumb closer to her index and her middle fingers revealing her anxiety, her hand barely shook. How can one say that she was beautiful without betraying her beauty? Her expression had that perfume from abroad that was an invitation to a thousand and one adventures of love. In turn, you were shipwrecked and embarked on her ship for the gentlest of crossings. It wasn't so much the light brown color of her eyes as their intense expressiveness. All the joy and all the pain of the world met each other there. What finally made me lose my mind was her way of curling up in her jacket or in her two arms crossed over her breasts, her legs intertwined in a double wriggling as if wanting to disappear from the gaze of others. As for the rest, she went through life with an unvarying and fluid swaying that, after the first emotions of the males, in the afternoon with the sun blazing down, made the commentaries about her passage fly.

She ignored, though, the salutations of the boldest among us, continuing on her way as if she had been alone in the world, leaving behind her a turmoil of rare amplitude. In the debate that followed, before a jury at the very least bewildered by the force of my words, I was the only one to defend her. Ordinarily, I was very reserved, never a tone above the others. Guys, you don't understand. You have just witnessed a Visitation. That girl, she's the transformation of Beauty into flesh! But, far from providing a better image of her, my defense did her a disservice. The guys found her haughty and distant. Disdainful, Amos gesticulated, adding a very pronounced grimace as well. No, but . . . what is she thinking, that skeleton? (Maïté was very thin.) I wouldn't even want her leaving prison. The object of merciless contention, her elegance would float like a mystery among us until dusk. In fact, Maïté would later admit to me that, while she was waiting to go past our little group, her heart was beating wildly at the thought that one of us might run after her. Something that, with a bit nerve, I would have done without hesitation, so much so was I under her charm. It wasn't difficult, though, to run into her again.

In her parents' absence, Maïté had moved in, along with her twin sister and one of her older brothers, with an aunt who was living in our neighborhood. That woman of some fifty years of age, who had seen me grow up and taken a liking to me, often lent me magazines forbidden by the son-of-the-man's policemen. We would often continue discussing them for hours and hours, to the point where the bigots of Temple Street would accuse her, in hushed voices, of corrupting a minor . . . When I knocked at the door, with the solid pretext of rendering a visit to her aunt, Maïté, having come to open it, couldn't suppress a crazy laugh. She surely hadn't recognized me. But the surprise of seeing her planted there, right in front of me, trying to find some kind of coherence in my stammering, could surely be seen on my face. In spite of her rather timid nature, she couldn't stop herself from asking me if the sight of her caused so much fear. On the contrary, I found the audacity to respond. Sometimes, too much beauty is disconcerting as well. My response bothered her. I felt it in the way she turned her eyes away, and I ventured even more. When her aunt arrived, without anyone having notified her by the way, I was still smiling. I had scored a point.

||||||||||||||||||||||||||||||||||||||||||||||||||||||||||||||||||||||||||||||||||||||||||||||||||||||||||||||||||||||||||||

during the night in steerage a new language is fashioned oh you hear during the night in steerage hands speak to each other discovering a language against the rolling the insistent noise of the waves against the hull of the big boat against the obscurity the hunger the stench during the night in steerage intermingling of language that brightens hope oh to illuminate the sign of dreams painting the return to the time before the pounding of the sea before the hate and the defeat the bird fluttering in the bush of memory our steps seeking rest at the foot of the tree center of the world oh life the hatch opens bodies hurried up top the blows of rifle butts to accelerate the pace *no time to lose* the animal follows a sailor garottes it constriction without retaliation the shackles have spoken the others pick up the language regain agility charge head lowered the animals are enraged in the tumult bodies clasp each other the captain shows up the wind makes the bowsprit's sail crack roars like a rifle shot several rifle shots mingling with the wind paralyze freeze dignity the time for the sailors backup firemen to put out the fire in their heads rifle butts smash against the shoulder blades the loins the chest don't leave any traces think about the presentation of the merchandise infernal clanking bodies hurried through the hatch

during the night in steerage blending of the new language oh mirage

||||||||||||||||||||||||||||||||||||||||||||||||||||||||||||||||||||||||||||||||||||||||||||||||||||||||||||||||||

When Maïté, no doubt less frightened because of my presence in the group, started to slow down her pace when she drew near us, I didn't know how to react right away. Thus, the jeers of the others followed me for weeks. On the one hand, they had maintained a certain resentment for her, even if they would have been able to cross Alaska naked from the waist up for a single one of her kisses; on the other hand, I hadn't known how to respond with the rapidity of a hunter. To my friends, I seemed scared, incapable of assuming my male role. As if the roles had been inverted and I had slipped into the skin of the prey. However, I wasn't born yesterday. I had even demonstrated an extraordinary precociousness in matters of love, a specialist, from my most innocent childhood days, in playing doctor and in stolen kisses on the cheek. My female cousins and little nursery school companions must remember that even now. But that, that was a totally different story. How could I get such a beautiful girl to fall in love with me? Even if I admired myself in a mirror, persuaded myself like the monkey in the fable, that nature, if it hadn't spoiled me, had at least not been unfair. Beside that, since primary school, I was always at the head of my class, but that didn't convince me. At that time, the girls were interested in guys much older, coming from distant horizons, superior on all counts to my comrades and me. They would visit them at the wheel of shining Japanese cars, the lines of which we admired enviously from a distance. That didn't stop us from avenging the scorned honor of the neighborhood by scratching the bodies of their cars with very pointed nails that we slid under the tires before sneaking away. As for Maïté, she preferred to respond to the timid, hesitant courtship of an adolescent eight months younger than she was.

Our first amorous rendezvous took place one Friday afternoon upon leaving our respective high schools. I had had to save up for two weeks in order to be able to invite her to the trendy cinema, where, under the cover of darkness, we exchanged kisses with such ardor that Maïté, who suffered from asthma, wasn't able to breathe anymore. I had never experienced anything like that before. Chills ran up and down my entire body. Enormous beads of sweat formed on my forehead. I grabbed hold of Maïté's hands and clasped her tightly in my arms while pronouncing her name in a hushed voice so as to avoid calling attention to us. The words fell from my mouth by themselves. Incontrolably. Maïté! Maïté! Maïté! I swore my love to her one thousand times. As if those repeated declarations could bring her back to the reality of our adolescence, there, in the middle of all those people indifferent to our embraces. My panic had the merit of eliciting a smile from my friend, more used to the disease's symptoms than I. It was then, as if lighting up the theater, one of the most dazzling images a man could be given to contemplate: her face, so beautiful, alternating between laughter and pain. We had to wait a long half hour before being able to kiss each other again. During that interval, the vows, floating like a breath of eternity over the dark movie theater, had replaced the caresses.

The following Sunday, with the complicity of a couple of friends, we'd met up on the hills above the city. Far from the hammer blows, from the filth of the city center, from the overwhelming heat. From then on, we took refuge there upon the slightest occasion. And we would drag out our kisses, like a slipstream of infinite love, in the fresh air among the majestic pines, the oaks, the mahogany trees, the mango trees. A surprising vegetation. An oasis of exuberance in the middle of the barren mountains that encircled the city. So many trees at once gave the impression of security. Everything was beautiful. Clean. The people. The animals. Superb horses were running about, mounted by Amazons who had come from elsewhere. Sometimes a man, clearly a servant, was leading one by its bridle. He would lead it with the deference of a person who was holding a sacred object in his hand. Paying more attention to the places where the animal was putting its hooves than to his own person. No pigs were seen. The houses seemed to have come from movies of enchantment. They were very far apart one from another. As if they needed space to flaunt their splendor. Immense walls three to four meters in height protected them, transforming the houses into impregnable bastions. Rare flowers everywhere. Orchids. Lilies. Begonias . . . Far from the noises of the city.

When she let herself go, Maïté called me her *sugar cane*. That nickname, a trifle exotic, would fill me with pride, had me wearing a satisfied smile on my lips all day long. I was far from thinking that the nickname constituted the visible part of the iceberg that would split the boat we were seated on in two. The first alert came with the sound of hammers that, born by the song of the unknown troubadour, resonated in the city day and night. To be sure, it was forbidden to talk about it, but everyone did. Some in the intimacy of their home. Others, more and more, in public, on playgrounds, in churches. Mimeographed journals were springing up like mushrooms without Titig and his henchmen being able to identify their origin: the writers, the printer, the distributors. They were passed from hand to hand, creased, crumpled. People hastened to read them; the most courageous photocopied them before passing them along to someone else who, in turn, perpetuated the chain of clandestine readers. How could I know that Maïté fostered a profound aversion for everything that could, either from up close or from a distance, remind her of her childhood?

She was two years old when all her family had to go into hiding to escape the persecutions of the police of the man-who-had-taken-power-for-a-thousand-years. Her father, whom she still didn't know when we met, was suspected of masterminding shortwave transmissions of a subversive nature from his place of exile. As a precautionary measure, the family had changed its name and stayed hidden away like rats for twelve long years. It wasn't until just before the accession to power of the son-of-the-man that she saw light again. Consequently, the day when, thinking I was awakening a vengeful streak in her, I brought her one of those censured journals, Maïté threw it to the ground with a rage that I didn't understand before disappearing without showing a sign of life for a week. That, in spite of the love letters and the gifts that I managed to get to her through her twin sister and that she would return to me with the same obstinacy. It was surely a question of seeing how far I was prepared to go to win her back. I had no trouble convincing her in that regard.

From then on, without clashes, we spun out love's sweet dream under the half-mocking, half-jealous glances of my friends from the neighborhood. They reproached me for snubbing them since that girl with cat eyes had brought her carcass here. You don't know us anymore. I would really like to know what you see in her, Amos asked me. Do her bones please you that much? My companions' grievances were not unfounded. In very little time, Maïté had taken a primordial place in my life. In her absence, every single one of my gestures was accompanied by a thought of her. Better, she determined them. And when I'd see her, I would drown myself in her eyes. (It's not surprising if, today, women accuse me of not putting enough effort into a relationship: Maïté took all the love that I had to give.)

In fact, she had become as indispensable to me as Grannie. The latter, with whom she would spend a good part of her time when she'd come over to the house, looked favorably, too much so even, on our relationship. But for her own reasons that I didn't want to hear anything about. She reminded us all the time that the wheel has turned, kids. Henceforth, God is waiting for me in his realm. Now that Maïté is here, I am approaching the other shore without any regrets. I'm leaving you in good hands, my little Jonas . . . Those words infuriated me, even if I was careful not to scold her. For me, Maïté was not there to take over for Grannie. I needed her just like I needed Grannie. Those two women provided an equilibrium for me that I hadn't known until then. Grannie was the roots, Maïté the branch that invited me, every day, toward new adventures in the sky.

IV During that entire period, when the trap of tenderness engulfed my adolescence, I lived as if detached from the rest of the world. The hammering seemed so distant, muffled as if in a dream. The song of the mysterious troubadour as well. I knew it by heart, though, from having sung it so many times at the reunions I attended without Grannie and Maïté knowing about them. Carnival rolled out its procession of glitter, its escapades, and its decibels on a distant planet several light years away from ours. I didn't hear the birds' vocalizations in the early morning nor the sun's cracking the corrugated iron roofs of the houses. Even the pestilence of the streets didn't reach my nostrils. I was living totally cut off from the world. As a consequence, I didn't see the big roundup coming that shook the city like an angry simoon stirs up the sand of the desert. The easygoing tiger had shown his claws.

More than one household was affected, accused of inciting the population to short-lived adventures. Applicants for departure and designated instigators landed in nameless jails where they would eat their own excrement in the darkness that enveloped their cries and reduced them to nothing. Some would never see the light of day again, reunited in mass graves discovered a long time after the events. That night the secret agents of the son-of-the-man burst in on a radio station broadcasting the song of the unknown troubadour while the microphone was still on. Everyone could hear the orders shouted over the airwaves, the slaps cracking, the salvos of the machine guns, and, in the silence that followed the departure of the ruler of the city's henchmen, the noise, monotonous and disagreeable to the ear, of a 45 rpm record having reached its end. The radio went silent, and with that, the whole city was barricaded in a fear similar to the one of those days of terror Maïté's aunt had often talked to me about.

Grannie told me about those days, too. After having double-locked the windows and the doors, plunging the house into semidarkness. She seemed to have hesitated a lot. I had never seen her in such a state of tension, of restrained nervousness. But you had to know, she said, and I had to inform you about the whims of your father. At least, you won't repeat them. Those things only bring tears and suffering to the families. That's how I learned the real cause of the disappearance of my parents. As far as I knew, they had lost their lives in an automobile accident a short time after my birth. That's what Grannie had always led me to understand. That day, she told me the truth. The whole truth. Papa's refusal to collaborate, his quest for a city open to everyone's aspirations. Those of the affluent as well as those of the lower classes. Unlike those of his generation, he rejected violence, even legitimate. He believed in education, the only thing capable, according to him, of giving rise to new men. To a new city. He had started giving courses for free and had transformed his house into an office of social assistance. Straight from the utopias of your grandfather, Grannie fumed. All that was quickly forbidden. Then, Papa made the decision to leave. Perhaps it was weariness. Perhaps flight, as some of his friends deemed it. The fear of arriving at an extreme solution, of closing his hand on the butt of a rifle and taking the life of another human being. In any case, he no longer wanted to make concessions. He didn't have the time, though, to act. One day, he vanished. Grannie hasn't seen him or Mama, who was accompanying him, again, nor the old car that earned him so much mockery from the kids in the neighborhood. All the measures taken to find them, dead or alive, were in vain, then, strongly discouraged when Grannie's tenacity led her into the offices of the lady, a distant relative, who administrated the unleashing of the hoodlums on the city. From then on, silence, like a pitch-black night, engulfed her suffering.

THE OTHER SIDE OF THE SEA

How old was I when Grannie related that story to me? The age when pain seems to have no hold on you and resurfaces many years later in the form of profound, tenacious wounds. The time of a memory, of a new drama in one's life. That day, by the way, confronted with the sobs, interspersed with hiccups, that shook the frail silhouette of Grannie, I had to interrupt her. I found myself, without exactly knowing how, behind her with my arms encircling her shoulders. My head was buried in her hair, from which a strong smell of *palma christi* oil emerged, the one she used to do her hair as well as to tan my body, to treat a serious wound, and to rub on minor transitory aches and pains. Since then, we have never spoken about it again. A glance, a gesture, even silence in certain moments of suffering or joy, took the place of dialogue in that regard. The few times when the reassuring absence of words made itself felt, the specter of fits of crying always intervened.

||||||||||||||||||||||||||||||||||||||||||||||||||||||||||||||||||||||||||||||||||||||||||||||||||||||||||||||||||||||||||||||

gnawing hunger climbing toward the head with the rapidity of a farcical monkey at the top of a palm tree pelting the passers-by with its projectiles sharp violent pains right in the middle of the forehead between the two eyebrows an iron bar that prolongs the nose wanting to stave in the skull rumblings of stomachs that respond to each other greet each other mistrust each other gargantuan rumblings on the one hand anorexic gur-gling on the other *cutting contests* of hunger the large intestines swallow the small devour each other attack each other in the stomach voracious pitiless bites the bodies become taut with pain grimace jaws are clenched the stomach idles secretes bile that mixes with nausea the mouth bitter the sharp pains that dazzle in the dark the head prepares to explode it explodes

noises of steps rushing down the ladder the hatch opens the day filtered into a ray of offensive light the bodies bellowing pieces of rancid bread and smoked herring tossed groping the paws are raised sounds of chains grabbing in full flight carrying immediately to the mouth some got some others didn't perhaps tomorrow

||||||||||||||||||||||||||||||||||||||||||||||||||||||||||||||||||||||||||||||||||||||||||||||||||||||||||||||||||||||||||||||

For close to a month, the city lived in almost total silence, penetrated here and there by some hammering followed immediately by blasts from automatic weapons. In spite of everything, rumors were running wild, spreading like the advance of a hurricane, all the faster in that they didn't emanate from anywhere. The hypotheses confronted each other as in a ring. Which one would have the upper hand? Was it a question of treason by the guards close to the good-natured tiger, the infiltration of extremely dangerous guerrillas, of people being fed up, the vengeance of the gods, which the regime, henceforth assured of lasting a thousand years, had forgotten to honor with its share of prayers and annual feasts . . . The son-of-the-man felt menaced and mounted a large operation against the sons of the most well-known men in exile. Just barely, the most righteous were saved. Titig would, by the way, benefit from the unexpected assistance of a good part of the population. Some, in fact, took advantage of the operation to rid themselves of a jealousy they had been harboring for a long time against neighbors, colleagues at work, or relatives. Others, to settle old quarrels that had lasted several generations: an unfair deal on a purchase or the extortion of a patch of land, a girl impregnated and abandoned as someone despicable by the person responsible for the wrongdoing, disgracing the race . . . For Grannie, all that was inevitable. When you see such events take place, the members of the same family haggling like dogs and cats, that means that the day of Son of Man is not far away.

Thus, Maïté and those close to her found themselves on the edge of a precipice. The smallest thing would be enough to send them catapulting into oblivion. For a while, her aunt imagined having them cross the Massacre River clandestinely and then rejoining their relatives abroad, but the risk was too great. It was better to watch one's step, to wait until the eye of the hurricane passes. Milk that rises ends up falling sooner or later. While waiting, Maïté and her family could count on a precious ally. By and large, the neighborhood, where the family's history was known, joined forces with them, a silent force, invisible but impenetrable. From that point on, Maïté didn't go out anymore, not even to go to class. Our meetings became less frequent for obvious reasons of security. I had to take a lot of precautions when going to visit her: pretend to be taking a walk, then slip surreptitiously into the courtyard before whistling the tune we had agreed upon. We spent long moments holding each other tightly without uttering the slightest word. Above all, you had to reassure Maïté, stifle her natural anguish. Her aunt and I succeeded rather well in doing that. But at night, I had trouble falling asleep. I would go to bed, my heart pounding with anguish. At any moment, you could expect a Jeep suddenly braking at your front door. For her and her family it would be a trip with no return.

Sometime later, rumors and official communications came announcing the end of the reprisals. In that way, the city learned of so-and-so's departure into exile, the disappearance of someone else, the internment of still another. All that amid the hustle and bustle—punctuated by the hammer blows that had rediscovered their rhythm—of the usual activities that had immediately picked up again. Like Maïté's going to school and Grannie's endless litanies. From time to time, the neighborhood's indolent rhythm was animated by the latest gossip: a wife's husband repudiated her after having heard that she had had a lover, but he himself felt free to cuckold her openly and publicly; right in the middle of the school year, a certain young girl of a good family had left for three months of vacation only to return with her features exaggeratedly haggard; the last son of the debonair one was a feline hybrid, his lion of a father was part of the dynasty's next of kin . . . In short, life had reasserted itself. Our love could, once again, flaunt itself for all to see. But the city would be plagued, for a long time after the events, with the aftereffects of that period when an entire family would disappear on a simple anonymous denunciation.

 Around six months after that event, Maïté came, all happy, to tell me her departure had been set for the summer. It appears that, over there, one can find work easily. She would work during her vacations and send me the plane ticket. I would be able to rejoin her very quickly. We wouldn't be separated that long. Isn't that true, Jo? Isn't it? For a long minute, I wasn't able to open my mouth. The Earth was spinning at a crazy speed. Dizzying. For two years, she had brought stability to my everyday life. Her life had espoused mine like a liquid the form of its container. She had been a lover, a friend, when Grannie was withdrawing little by little from the world, hurtling me, at times, into an unfathomable void. I had trouble envisioning our neighborhood, my life, without her cadenced walk, her waiting at the end of the day, our kisses that left us short of breath. I was, of course, aware of the procedures that would facilitate her leaving the city. Maïté had told me about them right from the beginning. We had even mocked them. But it was something different to learn it then. To know it for real. Especially since, tranquility having returned, such a decision could seem null and void. Premature, in any case . . . Waiting for a reaction, Maïté was standing there in front of me. A burst of joy. Tears. A hateful wail. But the Earth continued to turn at the same crazy speed. Was I happy for her? Yes, of course. You will be reunited with members of your family. She understood the trace of irony in my voice, bit the inside of her lips while staring at the tips of her shoes as she did when, faced with a delicate situation, she didn't know what stance to adopt.

From Easter to July, time had never seemed so slow to me and so fast at the same time. I wanted to savor each moment, take the fullest advantage of it. Every day that passed was as precious as a drop of water in the middle of the desert. Her guardian would close her eyes to our late return from walks, from the fair, or from the movies. She accepted our Sunday excursions to the beach although she had previously refused them with all the force of propriety and of what-will-the-neighbors-say. It was there, with the complicity of a bungalow shaken by the rumbling of the waves, that Maïté gave herself to me for the first time. In a total, convulsive quivering of our two bodies. That love, celebrated in the flesh, was a discovery for me. Unlike my relation with Marie-Claire, I wanted to give rather than to take. Offer something that could defy and conquer distance, the massive body of salt water, all the guard dogs over there.

At the same time, I couldn't stop myself from feeling that the trip was an act of treason on Maïté's part. An impression that would poison the course of the remaining weeks that we would spend together. So I withdrew into myself, tenaciously rediscovering my inner world, wishing the months were hours and the hours seconds. Preparation for the second part of the baccalaureate was the ideal pretext for not speaking to her for several days, days that passed slowly like those days during the rainy season when you'd spend hours sitting on the veranda watching the earth drink until its thirst was quenched, until it regurgitated the excess water, which would take possession of the street, empty except for the rapid passage of the rare pedestrians, pedestrians bent over, looking, in that ridiculous position, for protection against the drops that, in fact, nothing could stop, not even the umbrellas that, under the repeated assaults, were shriveling up, bending like a mango sucked to satiation whose useless peel was thrown into a ditch . . .

Maïté didn't know how to penetrate my silence. Cold. Glacial like the marble of a stele. Already not very strong, she was wasting away before my very eyes. Her guardian became alarmed. Was she having trouble recovering from a secret abortion? I don't want any trouble with your mother. You know that. Maïté had to swear to her that no, it wasn't that. What is it then? It's something else. In any case, you wouldn't understand. Racked by doubt, I took sadistic pleasure in twisting the knife in the wound. Out loud, I went into raptures about the big butts of the girls we ran into during the course of our walks. Maïté took it without saying anything, until one day she slapped me before running away crying. For a week, I remained champing at the bit and thinking about how to avenge the insult, all the more so since the slap had been administered in full view of two neighborhood friends, far away to be sure, but implemented so well, with a smack of such resonance, that they had turned around and seen me bring my hand to my left cheek. Since my friend visited Grannie regularly during my absence, she ended up waiting for me one night with a copy of one of the censured journals in her hand. The journal, along with her air of a martyr, dissipated any idea of vengeance. I took her in my arms and embraced her in such an impassioned outburst that she was stricken with a violent asthma attack.

|||||||||||||||||||||||||||||||||||||||||||||||||||||||||||||||||||||||||||||||||||||||||||||||||||||||||||||||||||||||||||||||||

the livestock linked in a long rope of suffering pushed toward the stairway that leads to the deck the violent light of day they close their eyes they reopen them several minutes later distraught they advance dragging their legs the chains' clanking the strange sound of their steps on the deck's wooden floor a short rubbing followed by the clanking of chains the steps shuffling along the wooden floor before they stop under escort in case those animals get loose and jump overboard it has already happened one mustn't run the risk of losing such an investment

they are on the deck a sun bath to kill the microbes the salt water to eliminate the stench the odor of mildew of vomit of dead rats the sailors throw a bucket of water in their face while holding their breath in the back on the chest the intimate parts they are disinfected marine salt is applied to the wounds left by the links of the chains the cadavers are brought up from steerage and with the help of a plank of wood slid into the sea the sharks haven't made the trip for nothing ever since they know they'll follow the big boat until its arrival the livestock is led back into its quarters the slowest are aided by a rifle butt to the shoulder blade the bottom of the foot in the back they trip put their knees on the ground get back up their tears blending into the blackness of steerage

|||||||||||||||||||||||||||||||||||||||||||||||||||||||||||||||||||||||||||||||||||||||||||||||||||||||||||||||||||||||||||||||||

Her departure came just before the examinations for the baccalaureate, which were postponed that year because of the demonstrations that were rocking the city. Maïté was wearing a rose-colored dress exactly like her sister's. Her collarbones were showing through below the neckline. Hidden under an elongated suit wherein all femininity was gone, her waist had completely disappeared. Her bony face was of a sad beauty. She had insisted on remaining alone with Grannie in her room, before reappearing an hour later, smiling. Outside, the others were getting impatient. When the car started, I was seated between her and her twin sister, while their guardian had taken the seat next to the driver. The trip seemed interminable to me. I wanted everything already over with, her not to be there anymore. A bit as if I had dreamed up this story. That she had simply been a bad night's sleep in my life. No one uttered a word along the way. The atmosphere was rather heavy. Because of my down-in-the-mouth look, for sure, but also because of Maïté's anxious nature, which fear had started to overcome: she was afraid of being recognized by the immigration police. I was still holding her hand, without saying a word, when we arrived at the airport.

The terminal was packed with people who were running in all directions: travelers, those accompanying them, the onlookers trying to get closer to their dreams. They called out to each other in loud voices, met up with each other, chatted for a while, luggage was being passed from one hand to another. A woman had arrived in a tap tap filled to the brim with suitcases of all kinds. Another woman was dragging a jam-packed bag ready to burst open. You wondered how she had been able to get it there. The Passport Man popped up from behind a pillar and came over to shake my hand. Be strong, my friend. In any case, only mountains don't move. I will come back to see you all. Once again, chin up. And he disappeared into the midst of the passers-by, taking his mystery with him.

The twins checked their bags in without too much difficulty, other than that of confronting those who arrived late and brazenly tried to cut in line ahead of the others. Maïté's sister took her hand like that of a child one is taking to school, and the two girls went over toward the immigration officer. The man stared at them warily, examined their passports from every possible angle (from a distance I could feel Maïté's heart exploding in her chest), leafed through an enormous register placed on the counter in front of him before stamping them with a noisy gesture and smiling at them, showing all his teeth. The twins then turned around to say good-bye to us for the last time. Maïté's eyes had the redness of an entire field of poppies. Her guardian and I stationed ourselves on the terrace above, in the middle of a crowd as numerous as the one in the lobby. From there we saw them disappear into the airplane without turning their heads around. A few minutes later, the aircraft had disappeared from sight, with the first love of my youth on board.

The world had just collapsed, but I didn't let anything show. Neither tears nor lamentations. Only an impenetrable mask that my older friend had the tact not to interrogate on the way back. In fact, it was the mask of a man used to seeing the people around him leave, pass from one side to the other of the sea, of life. Each time, it was a sort of caving in of the world that, scarcely having reestablished itself, had to face up to another collapse. Cherished or unloved faces, laughs, those presences that confirmed our vision of things suddenly stopped turning up. The departure of those near us always leaves a strange sensation. Like a bit of twitching flesh that someone had torn out of our body, then abandoned in a corner, not having had need of it. As a child, I didn't ask myself why those close to me were leaving. The injustice of it took the place of reflection. What could be better over there? Life on this side of the ocean didn't seem that cruel to me. In spite of some shortages I would have preferred not to have suffered from, and the progressive discoveries, coming during an afternoon or a morning, which would attenuate the impression of perfect felicity. In spite of the bravado displayed at each new disappearance, I have never really gotten used to them.

This time the blow was even more severe. And while the car was rolling along in the heat of the early afternoon, I was seeing the faces of those who'd disappeared, a slow melancholy projected onto the reflection of the road. Our return home was one of the strangest that I have ever experienced. I had trouble recognizing the neighborhood where we had been living for such a long time. The star apple trees, the almond trees, the Spanish lime trees, the oleander, the laurels—both rose and white—the hibiscus, the pomegranate trees in bloom, even the air itself, everything seemed suspended in a non-place and a non-time. My body floated outside of me, and I asked myself what I was doing there. In her absence. I have never again felt that sensation of being in a dream in reality itself. Maïté's departure left a long streak of suffering.

VI For a long time, that I don't remember anymore, our letters crossed above the clouds at a rhythm of two or three per week. Scarcely had I drafted a response than I had to do another one, even longer and more detailed. From then on, when the mailman honked from atop his moped announcing in that way a letter for the house, Grannie wouldn't even open her eyes anymore, nor ask the servant to go get it. Sitting in her rocking chair, rocking gently what is left of her life, she would merely shout, Jonas, it's for you. She hadn't finished pronouncing my name than I was already rushing down the stairway, before heading back up with the same stride, after having slowed down on my way past her to apply a sonorous kiss to her neck. That always made her quiver with joy. Back in my room, after waiting to catch my breath, I would undo the envelope with the precision of a goldsmith for fear of tearing it, even wrinkling it, and lie down on my bed in order to hear clearly Maïté's voice in each line. In each word.

The first photo was full of modesty. Like her. Hesitating between the lasciviousness of her half-covered body, lying on the bed, and the sadness of the expression. Desire and my absence on the same rectangle of glossy paper. I kept the photo with me for several days before I decided to put it in the yellowed album where Grannie kept, in the same sad order, the photographs of relatives and friends, departed or deceased. For those who were still living in the city, there was another album decorated with flowers, sometimes even sketched by Grannie's hand, wavering watercolors drawn according to the arrangement of the pictures as if thrown in there any old way. How many times I surprised my grandmother, her eyes full of tears, in the midst of passing photographs from one album to another!

Very quickly, it became necessary to organize elsewhere the

numerous photographs of Maïté that were covering the walls of my room. Her timid smile, her way of imitating her twin sister in everything, even the pose of a star wrapped up in a smile for a crowd of invisible admirers, accompanied me even in my sleep. I recounted for her the slightest events of the day, kept a chronicle that linked my personal history to that of the city, a chronicle in which the city would always end up getting the upper hand. Influenced by a history professor, I passed the competitive exam for entrance into École normale supérieure. Very few of my comrades had enrolled in the city's university. The others had chosen to leave. Sometimes even the day after the exams. The most fortunate ones had a position already waiting for them. Most of them were hoping to work three or four years in order to save the money that would enable them to take up the branch of study they desired. Some would succeed. Vegetating in a mediocre life on foreign soil, others wouldn't.

The noise of hammers had started to reverberate again, non-stop, interrupting sleep, interrupting conversations. Demonstrations against Titig, pushed to the limits of hope by the song of the unknown troubadour, were multiplying in the city. The situation was tense. No one went out at night anymore. No one ventured outside, even during the day, unless there was an urgent need: to get fresh supplies, to look for help . . . At a moment when no one was expecting it in the least, people started to run, as if seized by a giant panic. The administration, the shops, the university, the schools all ended up closing their doors, leaving the street at the mercy of the machine guns and the assault tanks. Only the cicadas, forced to, ventured out, the time for a stop at "To the Happiness of Usurers." The poorest, like those working in subcontracted factories for several centimes an hour, were reduced to boiled green mangoes. According to the oldest, the city hadn't known a similar crisis since the debarkation of the whites. Mistresses were angry with their lovers, who were incapable of finding pretexts for visiting them. The married women were jubilant and were paid every night, in cash, for the nights of want that they had had to deal with. The days of power seemed numbered. God had weighed it on his

THE OTHER SIDE OF THE SEA

scale and had found it light, ventured Grannie, whose tongue
was becoming a bit looser during the course of the events. Unless those were the first signs of senile dementia. In any case,
from time to time, she would raise her index finger and, with a
sententious air, utter in an unknown language, "Mene, Mene,
Tekel et Parsin."

My letters overflowed with enthusiasm, to such a degree that
I would forget to tell Maïté what was essential. At least what
was essential in her eyes. To formulate for her, in the flow of my
pages, those flattering words that nourish every relation of love.
The only ones capable of defying distance, of transforming the
immense ocean into a stream. For me, there was absolutely no
incompatibility. Telling her about the city, its convulsions, the
lunar taste of its dreams was my way of loving her. With a
sentiment as strong as that of the unfulfilled need for a father
who had disappeared too soon. She pretended to be annoyed—
perhaps she was suppressing her anger—made me respond to
precise questions. No, I haven't replaced you. Not in mind, nor
word, nor action. I would add as many phrases like that as possible, knowing that, even upon command, they would give her
pleasure. Of course, I miss you. Especially Friday afternoon at
the end of classes and Sunday when I happen to go to the beach
with my friends. Then, I am gripped by my nostalgia for you
with an unsuspected violence.

In response, she would send me long letters with very ironic
overtones: "To the man of my life who loves me more than poli-
tics." Entire pages talking about over there, about her first steps
in that world so different than here, the people she had met, the
friends from our neighborhood who wanted to have some news
about me. It took her a while to evoke her reunion with her
father. As if all those new names, superabundant in her letters,
could ward off his. Why such a silence? I ended up asking. She,
lapidary: a complete unknown who left her indifferent in spite
of his onslaughts of kindness. On the other hand, she had tears
in her eyes upon hearing him recite throughout the day, "When
will I see again, alas!, my small village/my chimney smoke?"
The man would die three days before the fall of the millennial
regime. Before the debonair tiger left like a thief in the night.

during the night in steerage the wide-open hatch like a poorly
closed wound words yelled in human language last stop hell the
livestock shoved onto the bridge the dazzle of the new sun the
big ship immobilized along the wharf the Christians the dogs
and the horses first the yapping of the dogs to greet their arrival
on this new land of hunting those similar stevedoring and serv-
ing as stepping stones

The city was one colossal clamor. Like one long, uninterrupted
orgasm. Carnival-like groups, who in this corner of the world
always seem ready for all the events, hit the streets at midday.
At the request of some fanatics, they improvised wild rhythms
with the song of the troubadour as their harmonic chord. The
women were offering their flesh to all comers, like one offers
a glass of water to someone thirsty. With generosity. In the ac-
commodating shadow of a tree trunk, of an ochre twilight, of
the night's noises. Even the most avaricious held an open house.
Champagne was mixed with rum and *clairin,* English tea with
citronella and cinnamon. How many days passed that saw the
population swimming in its sweat and its assorted jubilations
without their feet getting heavy for a single instant? For once,
the drums weren't heavy after the dance. Everywhere, the people swept, cleaned, pulled weeds in a spontaneous relearning of
hope. The hammering that pierced the tranquility of the spirits
had given way to a silence, new and forgotten. Men and women
started walking the streets at night again, drinking, partying,
conversing until the first signs of morning's light. But all that
will barely last the time it takes to think about it.

Subject, for a long time, to the caprices of the father and the
son, their former henchmen, who had, with a burst of pride,
introduced a false note into the slide of the dynasty, were going
to savor in turn the fruit of the exercise of power. They found it
tasty and intoxicating. From that time on, not a week would go
by without the city making the news in one of the international
newspapers and on television. And you saw those operatic gen-
erals, taking on a menacing air, bellow curses against imaginary

enemies and prophesy the installation of social justice in a vain effort to establish their power. But three months later, they were crossing the Massacre River without getting their feet wet, were thrown in a cell, shoved into an airplane, or assassinated. And the assault tanks, orchestrated by other dancing instructors, began their ballet in the city's streets again.

What role did the strange absence of Maïté play in that period of my life when the noise of the hammers, which had started again with its ancient relentlessness, resounded in our letters, even to the point of becoming their essence? From that point on, I wouldn't talk about anything else to my friend, who pretended to take an interest, as much as me, in the thousand vicissitudes of life here. Little by little, love withdrew from the shuttle of our words, transforming Maïté into an ear necessary to believe in all that. In the possibility of changing life into the dew of hope for all.

More than once, Maïté invited me to visit her over there. She couldn't leave, herself, as long as she didn't have a residence card. Otherwise, I would have already come to gouge the eyes out of that vixen who has changed you so much. To rescue you from her bewitchment. What's that stuck-up bitch's name? In fact, Maïté knew full well that there was no other girl in my life. Intuitive as she was, she would already have figured it out. That wasn't it. It had to do with something else. Stronger than love. Stronger even than the desire to tell her "I love you." With my words, with my penis. It was as if the city was going to collapse as soon as my back was turned. It was the desire to not go away, to not go to sleep in order to prevent the danger, like an unfortunate prophesy, from occurring. Maïté couldn't be unaware of all that. But it is always easier to fight an adversary your size.

At the height of my illusions, I wrote to Maïté to explain to her that my future was here in this city. On this piece of earth, arid from having cried too much. The city needed my youth and that of many others. I could bring my stone to the reconstruction of the edifice. Her response was a torrent of abuse and desperation at the same time, a scarcely veiled menace: "I hope that you haven't made a mistake, that your edifice won't crumble down on top of you. As for me, us two, we're finished. Thus, you will have lost both the crab and the sack." Nonetheless, we would continue to exchange letters with the same regularity, as if unable to separate one from the other. Because of too much love, or because of habit. Like the ocean, linked to its shores for eternity. Of course, Maïté didn't talk to me of love anymore. But, there was no doubt in my mind that, sooner or later, she would return to her native city. Return to me . . .

I don't know, in the final analysis, which one of us didn't respond anymore to the letters of the other. No doubt it was time, the waves that delighted in effacing our respective names each time we would write them in the sand on both sides of the ocean, the noise of the hammers that ended up drowning out our voices . . . I still keep under my bed, though, the two enormous boxes of letters and photos that, ever since, have been the object of so many threats of auto-da-fé.

VII The night of the disappearance, I was awakened by the hammer blows. Even more ferocious than usual. In fact, brazen, like the first day I heard them. Louder than the galloping of all the horses that were running through my mind. The house, my bed were shaking. The breaking of glasses flung against each other was probably coming from Grannie's old dresser. I sprang out of bed, leapt toward the window, whose shutters I threw open noisily on each side of the wall, and saw a flood of humanity rushing in a disorderly procession. No scene from Carnival nor from a stadium in delirium could be compared to it. The entire city was in the street. Men, women, children with, as all their luggage, a simple suitcase for one, a bundle for another, while others were empty-handed, but they all had the same strange expression on their faces, like a veil of fear and of immense joy at the same time. And that human tide was moving toward the sea. I turned on the radio and swept across the dial trying to find an explanation. I ran back toward the window. The crowd was still advancing, resolute, indifferent to everything that was going on around it. Some people were chanting, "Mèsi Bondye, gade kijan lamizè fini pou nou." The others were content with walking, their gaze, like those of zombies, riveted on the horizon.

Finally, the radio provided me with several bits of information. The rumor had spread throughout the night that, given all the problems that the city was confronting, the neighboring people of Gog Magog had decided to open their doors to everyone who wanted to emigrate. The principle had just been applied in another island in the region. The rumor had added that the administrative formalities could be completed over there. No one knew where the news originated, but everyone believed it.

The steps resonated with a muffled martial sound. The wall of the house continued to shake. I rubbed my eyes with both hands. Those wanting to leave were arriving from everywhere, invading the airports, taking the ports by storm, boarding the cruise ships and freighters, hopping on the first floating vehicle that came along. Toward the new Promised Land. More than one person extemporized as a sailor, without any knowledge whatsoever of either a compass or a navigational chart. People were ready to do anything for a place on board: prostitute themselves, sell their family and their soul to the devil, kill, by shoving into the water the head of whoever was desperately trying to grab onto an oar, an airplane wing, a propeller that would amputate their two hands as cleanly as a sugarcane mill . . . Those who didn't find means of locomotion didn't hesitate to throw themselves into the water, saying to themselves that they would end up getting there by swimming. Watching the humans leave, the animals, too, took to the sea: dogs, cats (God alone knows though how much those creatures are afraid of water), crocodiles, rats, cockroaches, ladybugs, hummingbirds . . . Specialists of the exodus proposed their services at exorbitant prices. The people who didn't move at all were rare: a few rich people, the new masters of the city, foreigners on bad terms with the law in their country, the members of diplomatic delegations, me, to watch over Grannie, who had vowed that she would only leave this land feet first . . . and the pigs, conscious of the fact that it would be impossible for them to find something better elsewhere.

The rumor gave rise to a clash of apocalyptic dimensions that would last an entire week. Tens of thousands of people perished: boats that had capsized, the physically handicapped, those who didn't know how to swim . . . As the hours and the days passed, the sea, so blue in this corner of the world, took on the color of red blood. Attracted by the feast, sharks arrived from all the oceans of the earth, some rare specimens unusual in this area: hammerheads, gilled sharks, dogfish sharks, porbeagles, mallet heads, sharks from the coast of France . . . , an innumerable variety, some of which sank from having eaten too much. Tired of so much human flesh, the killer whales started playing volleyball with the bodies. One saw human beings, propelled by the violent swats of a tail, bounding fifty meters above the waves and, after a few minutes of such treatment, falling back down, crushed, into the water. Having gotten wind of the exodus, foreign journalists showed up in helicopters and hydroplanes from the city on the border, for there was no longer any place at the international airport for a Cessna to land, not even the tip of a wing. Even the dirt runways, reserved for the dropping off of cocaine coming from Cali and Medellín, welcomed airplanes, coming from who knows where, that arrived here filled with reporters speaking languages that we had never heard in this area.

When the chief of staff decided to react, it was too late. The ordinary soldiers, those without rank, had deserted and gone, inflating the massive number of those leaving. Soldiers from the other side of the mountains were called on for help, and they were fidgeting impatiently waiting to intervene. They arrived with their billyclubs as long as the extended trunk of an elephant. The government of the Promised-Land-in-Spite-of-Itself wasn't long in reacting, either. It gave the green light to its naval commander, who launched dozens of gunboats filled with soldiers, armed to the teeth, with orders to shoot on sight. By all means possible, the invaders had to be turned away and the local population reassured since the presidential election was drawing near. The military, who couldn't have asked for more, took advantage of the situation to unearth some old biological weapons from World War I that were stagnating in steel vats dozens of meters underground and to test others differently than by computer simulation or in the desert. The warships were aligned in international waters, halfway to the Promised Land, in a triple curtain of steel, with their fire-breathing muzzles pointed at the beachhead of those dreaming of El Dorado. And without warning, they fired on the precarious vessels while airplanes buzzed right over them and covered them with layers of gas. But they continued to advance. In fact, the first ones hit paved the way for those behind. During maneuvers, while one row of warships was retreating to make way for another to take its place, men and women who only had one arm or one eye left succeeded in breaking through the iron curtain, all the more so since the death machines started running short of munitions. While they were stocking up again, millions of others, crippled by destiny, were able to reach the forbidden shores.

||||||||||||||||||||||||||||||||||||||||||||||||||||||||||||||||||||||||||||||||||||||||||||||||||||||||||||||||||||||||||||||||||||

livestock under escort shoved some howl how many moons for the trip to the unknown toward nothingness and the negation of the human tears furrow some faces others jump the sea welcomes them swimming furiously backtracking to over there the route of Elegba dogs released sailors thrown into small boats and rowing the sailors rowing hard into the flanks of hope most recovered with hooks planted in the neck in the small of their backs the blows of paddles others not two or three sinking straight to the bottom singing fettered by their chains sinking the route of Elegba without having seen the land not promised

||||||||||||||||||||||||||||||||||||||||||||||||||||||||||||||||||||||||||||||||||||||||||||||||||||||||||||||||||||||||||||||||||||

Moved by such determination and not feeling menaced in any way by those poor wretches armed only with their desire to live, the men and women of the Promised Land organized more pleasant welcome committees to go to meet them, snatching them from the soldiers who had come to welcome them as well. They established networks of generosity pompously baptized "A Planet for Everyone." Those committees saw to it that the new arrivals were dispersed all over the place so as to shield them from the investigations that, there too, weren't long in coming. The politicians called on the population to denounce every individual suspected of harboring an invader. Thus, the most active members of the association found themselves behind bars, hit with prison sentences for life for the crime of high treason against state security. Faced with the magnitude of the exodus and the means put into place by the Promised Land to counter it, the Emergency Council of the highest court of the planet met and decreed, at the end of three days and three nights of extravagant discourse, that every nation has the right to defend its borders. The human rights defense committees, wanting to gain time and delay the deportation orders, argued that the alleged invaders hadn't arrived at the borders of the Promised Land. The nationalists retorted that one had to nip evil in the bud. The governments of other promised lands, from the region as well as from outside it, sent reinforcements to the scene in order to aid the nations they had friendly relations with: one shouldn't create a precedent nor disrupt the status quo in the world . . . Seven days and seven nights which saw the sea tremble on its axes, overflow and invade the cities along the border. Seven days at the end of which the steel curtains, which had multiplied like jellyfish, were successful in containing the flood of invaders, leaving tens of thousands of cadavers. The survivors were accompanied back to their shores of origin, then several steel barriers, composed of as many warships, were deployed along the city's coastline.

While I was witnessing those maneuvers, broadcast live by a satellite T.V. station, Grannie passed out, holding her chest in her bony hands, her mouth open as if she couldn't breathe anymore. Each time she caught her breath again, it was to repeat, like a broken record, "I had to see that, too!" Seeing Grannie choke, I was petrified before I finally decided to react, to run into the kitchen and bring back a jar of cold water, which I threw in her face with full force. Nothing happened. Then I wanted to air out the living room. In search of air, nonexistent in the middle of the day, I opened all the exits. I turned the fan on full blast and directed it toward Grannie, who didn't stop gasping for breath. Her chest was rising and falling at a frenetic pace. Outside, carried along by the blows of the hammers that were increasing in volume, people were marching resolutely in the direction of the sea.

No one saw me rush into the street, elbowing like a ram in order to clear, with great difficulty, a path for myself in the midst of the crowd that continued to advance like an army put to flight. I ended up reaching my destination and barely caught our doctor, a distant relative, who was getting ready to leave himself, with all his family. The man didn't have any choice; I was already hanging on his arm, dragging him toward the exit. He grabbed his instrument case on the way out before following me. While running, I explained to him what was up. It wasn't easy to backtrack in the other direction. I had to cut through the mob while keeping an eye on my cousin, for fear that he would escape. When we arrived at the house, we found Grannie with her head hanging backward, on her left side, her mouth full of froth. Slumped in her rocking chair, she was gently rocking her departure from the world of the living while the television screen was still showing images of the exodus with a close-up of a young girl in tears, who was looking for her brother in the crowd. The doctor signaled to me that he was no longer of any use whatsoever and withdrew like someone who had seen a ghost.

 "This city is screwed."
"That's not true."
"Where do you see hope?"
"In the eyes of the people."
"Me, I see them pallid. The stares of zombies."
"They will wake up one day."

"When?"

"I'm not a seer."

"How do you wake them?"

"Have to give them salt to eat."

"There isn't any anywhere."

"Someone will go looking for it."

"Where?"

"I don't know. There must be some somewhere, at the bottom of their hearts."

"They're dried out."

"Somewhere else, then."

"Who'll get it? Who'll bring it back to us?"

"A Messiah."

"Do you still believe in that?"

"In the coming of Christ or in nondevelopment?"

"Both."

"I don't believe in that anymore."

"In what?"

"In Messiahs."

"Why?"

"They are badly disguised devils."

"And the development of the city?"

"I'm an agnostic."

"What's the connection?"

"It means that I have my doubts . . . You have to leave, my friend, go away. Put the ocean between you and all this shit."

"You know full well all that follows you. Wherever you go."

"Evil spells don't cross water."

"Who said anything to you about evil spells?"

"This land has rotten luck."

"You have to release its mystical powers, release it from its spell."

"I have never dealt in mysticism."

"What do you propose?"

"I'm taking off."

"We haven't said our last word yet."

"We've said too much about it."

"We have a glorious past."

"That's of no interest. Only the present and future count."

"Stay."

"No."

"We need you."

"To do what?"

"What a question! You graduated from the École normale supérieure."

"That's past history. The professors earn low wages teaching famished students. They earn just enough to feed themselves and dress decently. And even that, by multiplying their course hours, by dispatching the corrections like a poorly paid mass of thanksgiving."

"Not all of them."

"The rest are of no importance."

"Why then?"

"They're bourgeois."

"So? You still have to take them into account."

"They're not from here."

"Who said that?"

"Me."

"Why?"

"Their umbilical cords were cut with a foreign passport."

"What's the problem?"

"They're from elsewhere."

"Not all of them."

"That's not my problem."

"Are you going to leave the city to the whites?"

"It's not a city."

"What is it?"

"A place of no importance."

"And not even?"

"A pigpen."

And why are there the whites?"

"We're all whites in terms of power. And besides, I don't know anything about it."

"There's oil."

"They can take it and bathe in it; they'll become like us."

"Rare ores."

"I don't give a fuck."

"Precious stones."

"They can eat them. And let them exit through their asshole. I'm leaving."

"Do you really want to leave?"

"Yes."

"Why, then?"

"You people are mediocre."

"US."

"I don't want to be a part of you any longer. I leave you to wallow, to marinate in your shit."

"Being abroad won't change anything."

"You never know."

"There's no vaccine against it."

"I don't give a damn."

"Things aren't necessarily better over there."

"It's here that things aren't good."

"How will you manage then?"

"At least I will inhale different air."

"Don't go."

"I'm outta here."

". . ."

IX Jonas stayed up three days and three nights watching over his grandmother's body, not to follow any particular tradition, but because it was impossible to find a funeral parlor in operation. Sitting facing the cadaver, which he had not thought necessary to move from the rocking chair, he took advantage of the situation to think. From time to time, he would let himself doze off before being torn out of his sleep by the gaping void that was opening under his feet. The heat, intense and muggy, rendered cohabitation with the corpse rather difficult. The young man had trouble breathing, but he decided not to leave the corpse alone. He was watching over it like a prized possession, an object of inestimable value. Who would want the shriveled-up, foul-smelling corpse of an old woman? No one, in fact. In spite of those difficult times when the dead no longer had any right to respect. But no one was interested in the bones of his grandmother. Neither for science nor for magic. Jonas could have left, vacated the house with the doors open. No one would have come close to it. The stench alone would have kept the thieves at a distance. The same stench that seemed to give him a somber intoxication . . . At the end of three days, activity timidly started to pick up again. The sounds of steps, of voices. Of life. It was about time, for the stench of the city, where hundreds of thousands of those repatriated had congregated, was merging with the beginning of the body's decomposition. The formalities were not difficult to sort out. The funeral took place the same day in the presence of an aging Uncle Antonio, a very distant relative. Upon his return from the cemetery, Jonas's decision had already been made.

Where was he going to settle? He didn't have the faintest idea for the time being. Such a departure toward the unknown was surely similar to death, but he was ready to accept it as something natural. Life and death are two sides of the same coin. In the course of one and the same life, we don't stop dying: we're always afraid, always suffering. Unless we prefer a sojourn without surprises and refuse all invitations from the world beyond. By renouncing what he possessed—that is, everything and nothing at the same time—by abandoning his native city, dying in its dirty chaotic streets, its mountains, pounded and ravaged by the sun, its ragged beggars, its arrogant bourgeois, its triumphant mediocrity, he was hoping to find a new life farther away. On the other side of the ocean.

Thus, he was going to travel, to the countries where his passport didn't constitute a handicap, depending on the money he had in his pocket (he had concluded a good deal on the house), the possibility of finding work here and there, and the people he'd meet. He'd be bounced around from airplane terminal to the dock of a port, from bus terminal to train station, without necessarily coming to rest. Like a man in love who'd pass from one lover to another to escape the image of the woman he loved. Better, to remain faithful to her in her absence. The most painful or, who knows, the most agreeable, would be the traces of that first life that he would keep deep inside him. Like a perpetual reincarnation . . . As for the rest, he would see later.

Port-au-Prince/Paris/Jerusalem
December 1996/August 1997